What the Frack?

by

Dennis McKay

To John,

With Best Wishes,

Dennis McKay

Published by Precarious Books

ISBN 978-0-9929880-3-6

A catalogue record for this title is available from the British Library.

Many thanks to Indie Authors World for their help.

To the memory of my father, Captain Bertram Dennis McKay.

Requiescat in pace.

By the Same Author

Drilling, Killing, Love, Drugs & Mud

by

B.D. McKay

Chapter 1 – The Spinster

It was on a bright, soggy autumnal day that the man arrived. The leaves were decaying in quiet anarchy throughout the village. There was no wind. Nothing was moving.

But things would never be the same again.

A dull and ominous knock alerted Jennifer. None of the cottages on the green possessed a doorbell.

She opened her 150 year-old wooden door and there, standing in front of her, was a Scotsman.

'Could you tell me where the village brothel is?'

'Excuse me?'

The man had the appearance of an overgrown West Highland Terrier. He had shaggy hair, a shaggy mustache and shaggy clothes. He looked Jennifer up and down with warm blue eyes. He smiled.

'I'm looking for a brothel. A knocking shop. I want to…'

'I know exactly what you want to do,' Jennifer barked. 'And you won't be doing it in this village.'

'If there's no brothel, there must be a local woman who's a bit of a…'

'Not in Foxhole Down.'

'Come on,' he winked lewdly at her. 'Every village in England has at least one slapper.' He eyed her up again. 'Even an old spinster like you must want it now and again.'

'Spinster? Old? I'm thirty-four!' she yelled.

And with a grace, agility and strength that she never knew she possessed, Jennifer skipped lightly over the threshold, planted her left foot and, describing a beautiful parabola with her open hand, slapped the brute violently across his cheek.

They both gasped.

Jennifer's hand throbbed. She was certain she had broken her wrist. She wondered if she had broken his jaw.

His eyes flashed at her angrily. He drew a deep breath. Finally, he smiled.

'Now I know where the village slapper lives. I'll see you again, darling.'

And with the wink of a watery eye, he was gone.

Chapter 2 – The Artist

Success had bought her a Grade II-listed, 18th century rectory overlooking the loveliest village green in England. The coach house, added in the 19th century, served as her studio. In it, she concocted art from an alchemy of oils, sable brushes, stretched canvas and turpentine. She didn't make any money from this art. Anouska de Gaulle made money from other arts.

Her greatest work of art was, of course, herself. Anouska's hair, make-up, nails and Jean-Paul Gaultier skeleton print trench coat had been designed as carefully as her name. As she stood looking out of the window, she could sense how striking and beautiful a figure she was cutting. Even the smoke from her cigarette was rising at a just-so angle. Effortless chic took a lot of practise. She could have been a figure in a Jack Vettriano painting. The thought made her smile. He too had made a lot of money.

Confronting Disappointment was the art show that shook the world and made Anouska her fortune.

Confronting Disappointment was an empty room.

Many artists had previously exhibited empty rooms. The idea was an old chestnut. What was revolutionary was what Anouska didn't put in the room – and, more importantly, what she did.

She made it clear that the room would certainly not include anything that anyone had ever hoped for, yearned for or dreamed of. She left it up to their own imagination as to what they could expect not to be there. And she left no one in any doubt that, for a not inconsiderable sum of money, they were in for a big disappointment.

Anouska had suspected that she might be onto something, but nothing could have prepared her for what actually happened.

After years of being terrorized by their governments with threats, both real and imagined; after globalization, increasing insecurity, poverty, unemployment and hopelessness; after food riots, anti-capitalism riots and grab-a-pair-of-sneakers riots; after war after war without end; after snivelling, gloating politicians gleefully announcing that "there is no alternative"; after watching their civilisations shrivel and their rights evaporate; after witnessing the biggest transfer of wealth from poor to rich in the planet's history; after all this, and after everything else that they'd had thrown at them, Anouska de Gaulle discovered that the public's capacity for disappointment was virtually unlimited. She had granted them the freedom to be disappointed in any way they chose.

They turned up in their millions.

Rooms were hastily opened in major cities all over the world. Bank accounts were hastily opened too. The media, in full piss-take mode, went into Emperor's New Clothes overdrive. They interviewed people queuing up to go in.

'I'd be really disappointed if there wasn't a jukebox in there,' said a quiffed and tattooed hipster.

'If there isn't a urinal or a pile of bricks, I'm going to be absolutely gutted,' said her friend.

'If there's no kangaroo, I'm going to be totally crushed,' said a fat, depressed-looking guy.

'No kangaroo with boxing gloves?' said his fat happy-looking pal. 'Or no kangaroo with no boxing gloves?'

'I'd be quite happy if there was no kangaroo with boxing gloves. I'd never demean an animal.'

'So what do you think won't be there?'

'I don't think anything will be there,' said the fat, depressed-looking guy glumly.

'Me neither,' sighed his pal.

The mainstream media never got it. Neither did the metropolitan elite – in any metropolis. The entire stunt was ridiculed in just about every parliament which allowed its members to waffle on endlessly about nothing in particular, which is to say: all parliaments.

Things were best summed up by an elderly woman attending her first ever art show. 'I wondered what all the fuss was about,' she said, 'but when there's so much interest from ordinary people, there has to be something in it. And when I saw them laughing on the telly, I decided I definitely had to come. It was incredible. It was mobbed. People were wandering about in a daze. Some were crying. We were all completely deflated. But disappointment has to be confronted. There's no getting away from it.'

Needless to say, the rich wanted to confront disappointment all on their own. Anouska de Gaulle made them pay richly for that privilege.

Peering out through her leaded windows, Anouska inhaled her Gauloise cigarette deeply. Smoking performed a number of functions for her. Gauloises reminded her of Picasso, the ultimate rule-breaker, the man of remorseless logic. The aromatic quality of the smoke took her thoughts and her heart to exotic places, far beyond the banality of "here" and the oppressive stupidity of "now". She did not desire longevity. Every cigarette was a memento of death. Time was limited. She was burning through it. There was much to be done.

Anouska pulled the trench coat tight. She didn't heat the house until after dark. Cold air was good for clear thinking.

'Have you seen what's happening on the green?'

Trudi had appeared. She was what £70,000 pounds a year bought you by way of make-up artists. She was lithe and lovely, gamine and gorgeous.

'What's happening on the green?'

'They're putting a big metal fence around it.'

Anouska furrowed her Botox-free brow. 'That's not a good omen for anyone.'

Anouska drew Trudi to her and tousled her hair playfully. She looked into her dark and beautiful eyes. Their heads moved inexorably together and they exchanged a light but lingering kiss, full of promise for the night ahead.

Looking at the trucks, taking another draw from her Gauloise, Anouska remembered the real reason why she smoked.

'I think there may be some dark and decadent pleasure to be had.'

Chapter 3 – The Fugitives

Happy ever after didn't last very long. Jamie and Antonia's bouts of fantastic sex had quickly tailed off as they settled down to domesticity in a hacienda in Catalonia which did not have satellite telly. Then the battle of the nick-nacks commenced.

Antonia could not abide the merest hint of empty space. Any ledge or table surface had to be populated with some kind of ornament, usually one to suit her own horrific tastes, or even worse, one which satisfied her mother's. The hacienda was heaving with small, ornamental garbage.

Jamie felt as if the entire world was pressing in on him. He needed space.

The situation had been compounded by what had happened on Jamie's first ever trip to an offshore oil rig. John Webster, the universally-loathed senior Toolpusher had been bludgeoned to death and tossed into a pit of foul liquid; Jamie fell in love with Antonia, lost her to a randy roustabout, then won her back again; he discovered who the killer was and then let him go; he also discovered the whereabouts of John Webster's eye-watering fortune. If this was all that Jamie had done, it would have been a pretty creditable first hitch in the oilfield. Unfortunately Jamie thoroughly blotted his copybook by accidentally adding 60 million dollars' worth of cocaine to the rig's drilling fluid system. The said cocaine was being stashed by Webster on behalf of some Russian gangsters. This faux-pas had ended Jamie's fledgling career somewhat abruptly. As is traditional in such circumstances, Jamie had fled for his life. He went into hiding in Spain with Antonia and her nick-nacks.

Fetching the money from Switzerland had turned into a bit of a drama too.

He contacted the bank in Zurich and asked what ID they wanted him to bring. 'That is not how we work here,' said the banker airily. 'The account details and the passcodes will be quite sufficient.'

And so, on a breezy August day, Jamie pitched up at a private Swiss bank with an empty attaché case to take receipt of two million Euros in cash from a safety deposit box.

He had arrived two hours early and spent most of the time pacing the streets around the bank in a baseball cap and sunglasses, looking for any goons who could have been looking for him.

Zurich was awash with goons. Switzerland had gone right downhill.

Jamie sat nervously in a café directly across from the bank, with two enormous thugs sitting directly in front of him. He told himself that he was being paranoid. Thugs went on holiday too. But then they acknowledged two other thugs driving past slowly in a large Citroen. And then they started chatting. In Russian.

This was enough to send Jamie through to the toilet at the back. His rear end had gone into fight or flight mode.

Jamie collected the attaché case and a suit from the waiter, to whom he slipped 200 euros. He changed into the suit and walked out, straight past the goons and into the bank.

The bank was an oasis of calm and helpfulness. It wasn't that they asked no questions. They asked reassuringly vague questions. It was illegitimate finance's equivalent of hairdresser's small talk. They even gave Jamie a couple of stiff drinks. They knew their business.

Jamie took his time counting the money. He slipped sixty thousand euros into the suit. He'd made sure the jacket had big pockets. He checked his watch. He had eight minutes.

There was a small waiting room by the main door of the bank. It was for the exclusive use of those leaving. Apparently Jamie wasn't the only customer who liked to choose the time of his leaving.

The one-way glass afforded Jamie a view of the street scene outside. There was only one Russian at the café. The other was standing to the left of the bank entrance, trying to look nonchalant. Jamie's taxi arrived and took up a position to the right of the entrance.

The next ninety seconds felt like the longest of Jamie's life.

At 11:43 precisely, Jamie emerged from the bank. He made quickly for the taxi. One Russian was behind him. He could see the other crossing the road and hurrying to run in front of the cab, which Jamie was almost at. From nowhere the Citroen emerged. It cut across the oncoming traffic and blocked the taxi in.

Suddenly, Jamie turned direction. The Russian followed. Jamie ran across the road. A car coming from the left had to brake to avoid hitting him. On the other side a silver pickup truck stopped. Jamie threw the attaché case onto the flat bed of the truck and leaped in after it. The truck moved off at speed.

Jamie sat up and looked at the confusion he'd left behind: one Russian forlorn in the middle of the road; the Citroen reversing desperately and trying to follow; and one Russian in the back of the truck with him.

The terrifying thing for Jamie was that the Russian grabbed him and not the money. It was Jamie they wanted. It wasn't a money thing. It was a revenge thing.

The guy quickly overpowered Jamie, but then seemed at a loss for what to do next. He held on. Jamie had a great view of the man's fat face. His eyes were bulging. His teeth were gritted. His nostrils flared in and out as he breathed. He also had a great view when the truck ducked down a side street and stopped. There was a brief shock when the syringe went in. Then the Russian's features subsided into drowsiness.

The Russian was bundled to the back of the truck and levered over the tailgate onto the road. Jamie grabbed the attaché case and lay low on the truck. The two men who had been waiting for the truck got into the cab. They moved off once again. The unconscious Russian was blocking the road for the Citroen. It didn't matter. They had arranged for a stolen car to seal off the road at the end.

Jamie's main concern now was to avoid being robbed by his accomplices. It was a five minute drive to the train station. Jamie checked the rooftops of the buildings as they drove past. All were familiar. He was being taken by the agreed route.

The truck came to a stop in a busy street next to the Bahnhof Selnau. The guys checked around for cops and gave Jamie the nod. As if it was the most natural thing in the world, Jamie got up and jumped onto the pavement beside them. Shielded from view by the two men's bodies, Jamie dropped the cash through the window onto the passenger seats.

'As agreed, thirty thousand?' said the driver.

'Sixty,' said Jamie. 'I know you've got families to feed. And my associates know where they live. So no funny business.'

The men smiled. The driver counted. A nod. One of the men gave Jamie his train ticket. In seconds they were gone.

Jamie took the train heading south. No one followed him. He got off at Brunau and located his hire car. He was quickly on the autobahn and quickly out of Zurich altogether.

On the long, circuitous drive to the French border, Jamie was able to ponder on a job well done. He had been in Switzerland over a month. He discovered and befriended some North African immigrants in Berne. He did know where their families were, although his "associates" were more likely to be shopping for horrifically-decorated porcelain than for hard drugs or AK-47s. His threats had to have some substance, otherwise they would simply have injected Jamie along with the Russian. Crime, he had found, wasn't for the faint-hearted.

But Jamie had a deep feeling of satisfaction. He had anticipated everything that had happened. Sometimes it pays to be paranoid.

*

They moved house. Antonia was Catalan, so they stayed in the region. They found a farmhouse sited high in a picturesque valley. It afforded great views, especially of the road. You could see people coming.

Having settled in nicely to the community and to the house itself, things took a dark turn after six months.

Jamie, by this time addicted to surfing the internet, chanced upon a headline in a BBC local news site:

Mysterious Death of Cornish Fisherman

Looking up at him from the screen was the face of the man who had murdered John Webster. Scottie had been the derrickman on the rig. He was the man who worked most closely with Jamie. He was also John Webster's son. Scottie had killed Webster - in an attempt to save the life of a friend whom he believed Webster was bullying to death. It was a doomed attempt. The guy had hung himself in his room.

In return for Jamie's silence, Scottie had seen to it that Jamie and Antonia's details were erased from the relevant industry databases. He had also gone on the run and had ended up, improbably, on a Cornish fishing boat. It bought him less than a year of life.

Jamie hoped that Scottie had made the most of his year. Things hadn't ended well. A sentence in the report chilled Jamie's blood: "The body, which was found at the foot of a cliff, showed signs of prior mistreatment."

Scottie, apparently, had also relocated to a remote farmhouse. It didn't do him any good. He never saw them coming.

Jamie took immediate action. A mile from the house, he had sensors fitted which could detect a car approaching. Small cameras were fitted to cover the surrounding area to a radius of five hundred yards. Jamie also invested four thousand Euros in night vision goggles for himself and Antonia. Another six thousand went on a quad bike and two more on a shotgun.

'You're being paranoid,' she said, as they performed their first night-time manoeuvres. Jamie simply smiled.

*

They came under cover of darkness.

The alarm went off at around two in the morning. A car had broken the beam. Jamie and Antonia dressed quickly. As Antonia grabbed the emergency bag, Jamie checked the screen.

They slipped out the back and went up to the rocky outcrop where the quad bike was stashed. There they waited.

It took half an hour for the three men to work their way into position: two at the back, one at the front. The shooting started before Jamie knew it. What they were shooting at was anyone's guess. Jamie had killed the electricity inside the house. There was more shooting, lots of it. When the guys came out, Jamie had to suppress his laughter. They had succeeded in shooting one of their own number. The three were bunched together, one supported by the other two. They made a fine fat target.

Jamie hit the floodlights and let loose with two shots. The three collapsed in a heap. Jamie killed the lights and Antonia started the quad.

As they drove past the side of the house, the dazed and wounded Russians fired indiscriminately. There was a sharp ping. The quad jolted. Antonia kept driving in a straight line along an old track, as they had practiced many times.

When they got to the car, they were amazed to find a driver sitting on the bonnet smoking. Spotting Jamie's shotgun, he threw the cigarette away and high-tailed it into the bushes. As they passed, Jamie let loose with two shots and blew the wheels off.

They drove the five miles to the nearest village, where their spare car was garaged, waiting with a full tank of petrol and a trunk full of luggage. They used the garage lights to examine each other for wounds. Nothing. They hugged.

They drove to a luxury hotel in the Pyrenees, checked-in, and had the most intense sex of their entire lives.

*

Jamie and Antonia lived out of their suitcases for a month, touring the Iberian Peninsula. They settled in one of the traditional "white villages" in the foothills of the Sierra Almijara in Andalucia, renting an apartment next to the town hall and the police station.

The fugitive lifestyle suited them. There was something primeval about their existence. With danger lurking around every corner, they couldn't keep their hands off one another. Sex and death were a potent cocktail.

After one particularly gruelling session, Jamie lay back, feeling like a caveman. Propagating the species became fiercely urgent when you were liable to be eaten by a dinosaur.

'We need to stop using contraception,' he said.

'I already have,' Antonia breathed.

This triggered another furious bout of lovemaking.

For all their bliss, they knew that they were on borrowed time once again. Villagers had begun asking questions about their jobs. Everyone knew that they were too young to retire. They themselves were becoming sick of their leisurely lifestyle. When some Russian tourists showed up in the square, it was time for Jamie and Antonia to take action.

'I've had an idea,' said Antonia, one bright morning. 'It's a job where you keep moving about and where they'll never think of looking for us.'

'I told you, I'm not going into sales.'

'It's not sales.' Antonia looked away evasively.

'What is it?' said Jamie, eagerly. 'Some kind of surveying job?'

'No.'

'Engineering consultancy?'

'Not quite.'

'Something in finance?'

'Hmm...'

'International luxury hotel travel journalism?'

'Kind of.'

'Well …?' Jamie's tongue was almost hanging out.

Antonia straightened her features.

'We're going back on the rigs.'

'WHAT??!! Are you insane??!! It's the worst industry in the history of industries. They're all pimps, thieves and arsonists.'

'Hear me out…'

'I'm not going! We'll get back to the heliport and Russians will be waiting for us with baseball bats. Besides, it's like a prison out there. Without any of the perks.'

'I'm not talking about the North Sea, you idiot. We'll do land jobs. They are remote. Safe. There are parts of the world where Russians don't go.'

'I'm not going to Africa and I'm not going anywhere they cut peoples' heads off, and I'm not going anywhere that ends in –stan. And I'm not going to Australia either.'

'Relax. This job is in England.'

'England's full of Russians.'

'Chelsea's full of Russians. They never leave London.'

'Whereabouts in England?'

'Hampshire.'

Jamie's face softened. 'Hampshire? That sounds lovely. Hampshire's absolutely gorgeous.'

Chapter 4 – The Man Who Made Things

Long John Silver had visited him again in his dreams. A bearded peg-legged pirate in a greatcoat, with that shrieking bloody parrot on his shoulder.

'Pieces of eight! Pieces of eight!'

Money. Alan had made enough of it. And he had made it by making things. It was an honourable tradition.

Tradition was important to Alan Wheeler. He was in the fortunate position of being able to look out on the same village green he had looked out on as a child. He was living in the same house. He'd never moved. He belonged to Foxhole Down.

His ambition as a child had been to be big enough and strong enough to push the roller which kept the cricket square flat. The day, aged 14, when he had been able to push it out, roll the wicket and return it next to the pavilion, had been the day he became a man.

He had spent the better part of his adult life rolling that grass. He always started in March on a dry, generally cold day. He followed the old maxim that half a day's rolling at the right time was worth a month's at any other time. If he couldn't do it at the weekend, he'd take a day off and let his company run itself. He'd spent countless contented summer evenings rolling, generally rounded off by a rewarding pint at the Royal Oak.

Foxhole Down's cricket pitches had been the truest and fastest in Hampshire.

It was fifteen years since there had been a village cricket team, five since a game had been played. Property had gotten too expensive for families. There was a lack of young men, a bit like after World War I. It was sad. The well-to-do who moved into the village wanted to look out onto a green, but they had no idea how to maintain it as a living thing. It was hard enough these days just getting the grass cut.

Alan was 76 now. His rolling years were behind him, his company sold. He'd never married.

He blamed Anouska what's-her-face for the Long John Silver dreams. She'd organised a fancy dress ball in the rectory. She'd invited the entire village, although it had been attended in the main by her fancy London friends. At least she'd made the effort to put something into the community. She'd received scant support.

The theme of the party had been "my hero". Alan had gone as Scott of the Antarctic. There had been three Hitlers, two Stalins and a Vlad the Impaler, but that was London for you. Anouska had come as Long John John Silver. She wore a magnificent greatcoat, impressive whiskers and a real parrot. She had a fabulous pair of thigh-length boots, although she had started with just one - before she got tired of pretending to have one leg.

It was in her one-legged state that she gave Alan the strangest look. It was as if she knew.

Then she had hobbled over on her crutch, smiling. 'Har har har! Alan me old shipmate. Let's spend some of our ill-gotten pieces of eight on some grog before we tip the Vicar the black spot.'

But if anyone had been tipped the black spot that night it was Alan, who remembered the character who had first turned up with a black spot. That was Blind Pew, the scariest man he'd ever encountered in a book. You heard him coming. Tap tap tap. He was blind, he hung around with pirates - and the pirates were scared of him. He stank to high heaven. And once he had a grasp of you he never let go.

There was a tap tap tapping at Alan's unconscious. It wasn't Blind Pew. It was another cripple, a portent that Alan's chickens were coming home to roost. Long John Silver cast a long dark shadow. And the bloody parrot couldn't be silenced.

'Pieces of eight! Pieces of eight!'

Alan's sense of dread deepened when he saw the fence going up around his beloved green. His instincts told him that something truly awful was being visited on the village.

There was only one place to go in such a crisis. Alan put on his coat, scarf and cap and made directly for the pub.

Chapter 5 - The Property Developer & The Conspiracy Theorist

Pub culture in Britain was dying. The smoking ban had been the final nail in the coffin. Or rather, the smoking ban had been the fatal stab to the throat that would put pub culture in the coffin that would be nailed down and buried in a grave marked: "Here lies Pub Culture. Died of neglect in an age of individualism. Beloved child of Neighbourliness and Friendship, who went missing sometime in the late 20th century. May they rest in peace with a fag, a pint and some warm conversation around a roaring fire."

Major Tommy Harris had twenty years of falling beer sales to tell him that he was slowly going out of business. It was only the food at weekends that was keeping him going. He was going to give it another couple of years and then he was going to turn the entire building into flats.

The pub was worth more as a property development than as a pub.

The Major was going to give it another couple of years. He liked people and he liked the banter. He thought of himself as the village therapist. Some people thought he was the village idiot. Still, it was all good fun and things had perked up a bit with the arrival of an internationally acclaimed artist in the rectory. She'd become a regular, arriving at around 5pm. She either looked utterly glamorous in full dress mode, or utterly artistic in paint-spattered old clothes and boots. Either way, she was up for a laugh. More importantly, she had brought in lots of her cosmopolitan friends. They liked to see local yokels in their natural habitat.

The Major had had a good Falklands War. In the Catering Corps. In Aldershot. When the time came for his demobilisation, he felt that he might struggle to make a living in the civilian economy. There could be but one destination for him. Pubs and majors went together like whisky and soda.

He'd been glad to have had the 80's and 90's to pay off the mortgage. Things then were still vibrant and gastropubs were far in the distance. What had really killed things were the incomers. They didn't know how to live in a village. They arrived with their supermarket shopping, shut themselves up in the house and surfed the internet with a glass of wine. The village shop has closed eight years previously. The church wouldn't outlast the Vicar. And the Major was calling last orders on the pub.

When the Major saw the truck unloading and the fence being erected around the green, he knew who would be first through the door.

The Major poured a pint of real ale. A fat, nervous, geeky man burst in. His arms were going in all directions – and so were his legs. His name was Grassy Knoll.

'They're fencing in the green! The workmen don't know who they're working for. They've no paperwork.'

Grassy handed over his own paperwork – a fiver. His only pause for breath was as he took nervous sips of his beer.

'This is major, Major,' he panted. 'They're typical capitalist lackeys. Blindly following orders. They're so far down the chain of command they've no idea who the evil force behind this is.'

'You must be the only revolutionary I know who has his own share dealing account,' said the Major.

'Just because it's a racket doesn't mean I can't be in on it. I trade so that I don't have to prostitute myself in the labour market. I'd rather rip the system off than be ripped off by it.'

Tom could see the wheels turning in Grassy's head, even as he spoke. He was nothing if not a multi-tasker.

'It's going to be a housing scam. More zombies for the village. They'll make millions. Leave about ten square metres of grass in the middle and call it a "sustainable development". Stick a wind turbine on it for good measure. A couple of solar panels. A bit of underground car parking. Some architect will be creaming himself as we speak.'

'I thought it was common land?' said the Major.

'Pah! Common land is about as common as common decency.' Grassy was in full acid flow. 'They've been dismantling the Magna Carta. We're headed back to the Dark Ages.'

'Pork scratchings?' The Major proffered a packet.

Grassy shook his head. 'I bet you that our corrupt MP is up to his neck in this. With his Russian gangster pals. This country has got the best government that roubles can buy.'

'We've a lovely soup on today. Broccoli and stilton?'

Grassy shook his head. 'Don't even think about protesting. Before you know it, they'll have you in leg irons and an orange onesie. Then they'll stick you on a rendition flight to Guantanamo Bay, where you'll be waterboarded and force-fed Mom and apple pie. And they'll call it "the prevention of terrorism".'

'Today's specials are mussels in a white wine sauce and beef burgundy.'

Grassy thought for a moment. He shook his head. 'It could be even worse than houses. Toxic sludge dump. Nuclear reprocessing plant. High security prison. One thing's for sure: they're going to be breaking turf.'

It was at this point that Alan came in. He promptly burst into tears.

*

'I've never cried in public in my entire life,' said Alan.

'You must have been a quiet baby,' said Grassy.

The Major shot a sharp look at Grassy.

Grassy changed tack. 'You're amongst friends Alan. We won't tell a soul. There's nothing wrong with tears.'

'It wasn't the way I was brought up,' sobbed Alan.

'Don't be ashamed. I've seen the toughest men crack under pressure of battle,' said the Major, who'd seen countless squaddies cry under the merciless pressure of peeling onions.

'You've put your life into that grass,' said Grassy. 'Those were the best cricket pitches in England. If it wasn't for you it would be completely overgrown.'

'I thought I'd look out onto that green until the day I died,' said Alan.

Alan swirled the brandy that the Major had given him. His hands were shaking quite badly.

Anouska blazed in, looking every inch the saviour of the moment.

'Champagne Major!' she cried. 'I must have champagne.' She strode toward the bar. 'Oh don't look at me like that. It's only idiots who drink champagne to celebrate. When you're down, it's the best drink ever.'

She clasped Alan to her bosom, knocking his cap off and spilling his brandy.

'Alan,' she breathed, 'I will die before I allow them to disturb a blade of that green.'

The champagne did make them feel better. They took Alan's brandy away from him – they didn't want him going home drunk and having a fall.

Anouska had a few conspiracy theories of her own. 'This has got council fingerprints all over it. It's Big Government if ever I saw it. You can't put a fence up around a village green without council say-so. The council are almost as left-wing as the Conservative party.'

If Grassy Knoll was an extreme left winger, it appeared that Anouska was an extreme right winger. It didn't matter. They somehow met around the back and agreed with each another – albeit for completely opposite reasons.

'I know you're all feeling disappointed right now,' Anouska continued. 'Let me tell you that there are great things you can do with disappointment. I should know. I've made a fortune out of disappointment. Disappointment has been my greatest success. You have to confront disappointment. Life is disappointment. It starts in tears and ends with a sigh. Everything in between is one big let-down. Once you've come to terms with that, the possibilities are limitless.'

'The possibilities for disappointment are limitless,' said Grassy Knoll glumly.

'Exactly,' said Anouska.

The company pondered this.

'So,' said Alan, 'are we preparing for the worst but hoping for the best? Or are we hoping for the worst but preparing for the best?'

'If we're expecting to be disappointed,' said the Major, 'we'd better raise our expectations. That way the disappointment won't be half as bad.'

'It'll be ten times worse,' said Grassy Knoll. 'If you want to lower your disappointment, you better lower your expectations. But that's what the capitalist oppressors want you to do. It's only by raising expectations that we can create the enormous disappointment that will ignite the revolution.'

'All revolutions end in disappointment,' said Alan.

'Hanging on in quiet desperation while your village is destroyed doesn't end so well either,' said Grassy Knoll.

'It seems to me,' said the Major, 'that we need to decide how big a disappointment we should expect. And how big our expectations of that disappointment are.'

All eyes turned to Anouska.

'Now you know why I created my exhibit,' Anouska sighed. 'It seems to me there's been a crisis of philosophy. At the present moment my philosophy is: more champagne.'

The delightful sound of the champagne cork popping lifted their spirits. The Major charged their glasses - even Alan's.

'Let's go confront disappointment,' said Anouska.

She led them outside.

'Now that's disappointing,' said Grassy Knoll.

The remaining pieces of fence were being slotted into their concrete bases. The encirclement of Foxhole Down's ancient village green was almost complete.

'Even Hitler never managed that,' said Alan.

'Unconquered since 1066. A thousand years of freedom. And now this. Not a bullet fired. We're doing this to ourselves,' said the Major.

'How much freedom we've had in the thousand years is debatable,' said Grassy Knoll, 'but I take your point.'

'They've even encircled the trees,' said Anouska, as the last piece of fence was kicked into place.

It was true. The northern and western sides of the green were populated by large, old and very beautiful oak trees.

'It's like the Red Army surrounding the Germans at Stalingrad,' said Alan.

'Do you have to use military metaphors for everything?' said Grassy Knoll.

Anouska looked sadly at the fence. 'If that's not a declaration of war, I don't know what is.'

The workmen, entirely oblivious to the devastation that they were causing, began attaching plastic signs to the fence with cable ties. They put one right in front of the pub. It read: This sight is protected by FUNdamental Security

'I bet they're a criminal organisation,' said the Major.

'We need more champagne,' said Anouska. 'In pint glasses.'

They went inside.

*

As she paced around in her coat and boots, Anouska looked every inch the General. The pint of champagne somehow added to the effect of manly swagger – with a definite feminine touch.

'Gentlemen,' she began. 'War has come to Foxhole Down. This will be our Battle of the Somme. As those did before us, so shall we stand firm. And endure. Our enemy will be implacable. And vicious. We don't even know who we're fighting yet.'

Jennifer stormed in. 'They've fenced off the green! A horrid Scotsman knocked on my door looking for a brothel. And he called me "an old spinster".'

She burst into tears.

'Give her a pint of champagne,' said Grassy Knoll.

'Could I have some ice for my hand?' said Jennifer. 'I slapped the Scotsman.'

The men cheered.

'Well done that girl,' said Alan.

'First blow struck for the village,' said the Major.

Anouska paced around, deep in thought. 'A Scotsman you say? Looking for a brothel? Was he Aberdonian by any chance?'

'I wouldn't know,' said Jennifer sheepishly. She always found Anouska a bit intimidating.

'You think he's an oil worker?' said the Major.

Anouska came to a stop. 'Oh my God. We're being fracked.'

Chapter 6 – The Member of Parliament

Jennifer vowed never to drink champagne by the pint ever again. Anouska had given her a small bottle of schnapps and told her to put it in her freezer. She may have loomed large as a fearsome character in Jennifer's psyche, but Anouska knew her alcohol. A belt of schnapps in the morning put Jennifer back on her feet.

The previous night's events had ended in predictably hazy circumstances. The company had vowed to fight to the death, but it had been left, inevitably, to the women to take the first action. Jennifer was to enlist the help of her distant relative, the local MP. Anouska was to enlist the help of the scariest man in the village.

As Jennifer tied her scarf and straightened herself up in front of the hall mirror, she was confronted by the old spinster staring back at her. There was no grey in the shoulder-length auburn hair that she tucked neatly under an Alice band. There were, admittedly, some fine lines appearing around her eyes and lips. Had her comfortable lifestyle merely served to protect her from life itself?

She thought back to the incident with Scottie Dog the day before: his arrogance; the sheer effrontery of his request; the utterly filthy way he'd looked her up and down, as if measuring her for his bed; the cheeky look on his face; the life-affirming pain that shot up her arm as she struck him; the confusion and hurt on his face; the way he quickly re-asserted himself; the adrenaline rush as she stormed triumphantly back to her kitchen to put ice on her wrist and make a strong cup of tea.

The awful truth was that it had been the first sexual attention she'd received in seven years.

Her heart sank at the thought. Her sexuality had lain buried under a heavy cloak of contentment. Since when did men have anything to do with contentment? She'd gone to bed drunk and distressed, but she'd gone to bed thrilled as well. How she longed to be longed after, the way that men longed after Anouska. Jennifer could only dream of being with the kind of edgy, urbane men that hung on the artist's every gesture. Jennifer had waited too long for a knock at the door. It was time for her to knock on some doors of her own.

It was easy for Jennifer to access her MP. He lived in the woods nearby. An early telephone call arranged a meeting for that very morning. Jennifer walked to her appointment. As she climbed the down, she stopped to take in the view. The village was heartbreakingly gorgeous. She felt incredibly lucky to have lived her entire life in a place of such undeniable beauty. It wasn't simply that the flora and fauna were perfect, it was the fact that the human impact on the landscape had been made so harmoniously. The houses, the roads, the church, were proportionate. They sat naturally in the landscape, surrounding the man-made village green, which was lovely in its own right. Jennifer felt her heart soaring. Tears pricked her eyes. This was the land to which she belonged. If Foxhole Down wasn't worth fighting for, nothing was.

The fence, glinting in the sunlight, formed a thin silver scar surrounding the green.

Jennifer took a deep breath. Emboldened, she turned and strode on toward a fateful meeting and a connection with the power of the realm.

Sir Benjamin Latham MP lived quietly and graciously in a somewhat damp abode surrounded by trees. His Edwardian pile in the woods was furnished almost totally in the Laura Ashley style. But it wasn't Laura Ashley at all. Sir Benjamin used exclusively French designers. He found the French version of Englishness to be more English than the English version of Englishness.

He and Jennifer had two things in common: blood and property. They were distantly related, third or fourth cousins. Sir Benjamin's property portfolio was larger and more London-centric than the handful of high-end local dwellings that provided Jennifer with a living. What was important about the genes, bricks and mortar was that they placed Sir Benjamin and Jennifer firmly in the same caste.

Sir Benjamin's wife brought the coffee tray through to the solarium. She exchanged some pleasantries with Jennifer and then retired to resume combat with a stew on the Aga.

Sir Benjamin entered in his Jermyn Street finery and half-moon glasses - a shining, silver, opulent creature in his sixties.

'Jennifer,' he beamed. 'Little cousin. Come and give your big cousin a big one.'

His arms were open. Jennifer assumed he meant a hug. They embraced. He squeezed her just a little too tightly. Two instances of male attention in under a day – after a seven year drought. She was on a hot streak.

'Jennifer darling,' Sir Benjamin beamed, 'you need to stop rationing your gorgeousness. We see so little of you.' He threw himself languidly onto his violet-bud patterned sofa. Serving the coffee was women's work.

Jennifer poured. 'I think we'll be seeing much more of one another.'

'Fabulous. Tell me, how's the raunch factor in your love life these days?'

'Definitely on the up. Why only yesterday I was offered sex on my own doorstep. By a Scotsman.'

'A Scotsman? In Foxhole Down? Hmm. Sounds like a stray ghillie. They come down here on their holidays you know. An offer of sex you say? What did you do?'

'I slapped him.'

'Sent him homeward to think again. Top girl.'

'I don't think he was ghillie, though. I think he was an oilman.'

'What made you think that?'

'He was looking for a brothel.'

Sir Benjamin let out the kind of dirty laugh that only men can manage, especially when women are the butt of the joke. Jennifer felt her under-developed feminist hackles rise.

'He's a bit late,' Sir Benjamin chuckled. 'There hasn't been a house of ill repute in Foxhole Down since the Corn Laws were repealed. I believe that one was alluded to in the Domesday Book in 1086.' He tapped the side of his nose conspiratorially. 'Reading between the lines, if you know what I mean.'

Jennifer knew exactly what Sir Benjamin meant. He had made a career of reading between the lines. When the MPs expenses scandal hit, he acted quickly to ensure that the talk was all about other peoples' duck ponds, moats and pornographic videos – and not his own croquet lawn, gazebo or ballerina in a Bayswater apartment.

'Does the flat in Bayswater still have that lovely live-in housekeeper?' Jennifer asked innocently.

Sir Benjamin gave a beatific smile, glancing slyly at the door to see if his wife had heard. 'Of course,' he purred.

'I hear that she dances very well. For a housekeeper.' Jennifer felt her lips pursing together.

'You really shouldn't pull faces like that, darling,' Sir Benjamin smarmed. 'It makes you look matronly.'

'You should have seen the face I pulled when I saw them throwing a fence up around the village green.'

'How strange. Who would do such a thing?'

'Who would allow such a thing?'

'Quite. I suspect it will be a tree thing. Dutch elm disease.

Or whatever the modern version is. Sadly there appears to be no shortage of tree viruses these days.'

'You think they're quarantining the trees on the village green?'

'What else could it be?'

'Fracking.'

'Someone's got a fertile imagination.'

'It was Anouska.'

'Now there's a girl I'd like to get to grips with.'

Jennifer felt another lip purse coming on. 'Unfortunately, you're going to have to get to grips with me first,' she said. 'And not in a way you'd like.'

'Steady on, Jennifer. Let's not get ahead of ourselves.'

'I need you to tell me what's going on, Benjamin.'

'I haven't a clue what's going on.'

'But you're the Member of Parliament!'

'What does that count for these days?'

'If this is fracking, you need to tell me now. Benjamin, look at me. Is it fracking?'

Sir Benjamin squirmed in his sofa. 'Not necessarily.'

'For goodness' sake. Are you really telling me that you don't know?'

'This fracking thing has a mind of its own. It's all laid down in law. No one can stop it.'

'But they're supposed to do it somewhere horrid and far away. Like Essex. Or Newcastle. If we can't protect Foxhole Down, what is the point?'

'I quite agree. But it's all geopolitical, apparently. It's bigger than you. It's bigger than me. And I'm afraid that it's bigger than Foxhole Down.'

Jennifer could now feel her cheeks burning. 'Tell me one thing, Benjamin. Just what, exactly, are you claiming to represent?'

'My first priority is to look after the security of all my constituents.'

'By destroying the very land they live on?'

'Nothing's going to be destroyed. Oil's running out. If we don't extract every drop, we'll be beholden to Russia. And you wouldn't like them to have their wicked way with you.'

'So we've to let you have your wicked way with the village green instead?'

'It's nothing to do with me.'

'Who is it to do with?'

Sir Benjamin shifted shiftily in his sofa.

'Benjamin ..... ?'

'That's not an easy question to answer.'

'Please tell me that you're joking.'

'It appears to be some kind of outfit operating out of the British Virgin Islands, related to another company from Bermuda, which is wholly-owned by some chaps from the Cayman Islands via Jersey. And there the trail goes a bit cold. But I'm sure that it's all above-board.'

And with a grace that surprised her for the second day in a row, Jennifer leapt up, skipped lightly across the solarium's flagstones, planted her left foot and, describing a beautiful parabola with her right hand, belted Sir Benjamin Latham across his fat chops.

'Benjamin, you are a complete and utter arse!'

'I keep telling you, it's nothing to do with me!'

'My property portfolio could be ruined. I could be ruined.'

'Fracking's perfectly safe.'

'Who told you that? Your new-found Cayman Islander friend?'

Sir Benjamin shifted some more.

'You've taken money, haven't you?'

'I haven't taken a penny!'

'No Benjamin, your pennies come from elsewhere. Did they give you a bung from Lichtenstein?'

'I resent that. I would never accept anything as vulgar as a "bung". I don't know what kind of company you've been keeping, but you need to mind your language young lady. You're creating a scene. Now sit down.'

Jennifer stood her ground.

Sir Benjamin took a sip of coffee. His hand was trembling.

'Now listen Jennifer,' he began. 'Our energy security is of the utmost importance to the freedom of these islands and our wonderful islanders. There will be some disruption to the village – for a couple of months. There will be some trucks. They will come and go in daylight hours only. There will be a little drilling noise, but that will be kept to a minimum. The generators will be silent ones. The water supplies will be scrupulously monitored and protected. Fracking, if there is to be any, will be conducted under the strictest controls. Once the well is complete, there will be a small installation of ten square metres, which will be hidden by shrubbery. It's a small inconvenience to pay for freedom.'

'Surely, there must be another way?'

Sir Benjamin adopted his most serious tone. He held a hand up. 'There is no alternative.'

'But we need a full enquiry. The villagers need to be consulted. We have rights. It's in the Magna Carta.'

The hand went up again. Sir Benjamin closed his eyes solemnly and shook his head. 'No turning back.'

Jennifer looked at this languid, complacent, expenses-fuelled character, ensconced in his dubiously-funded, tastelessly decorated natural habitat. The man would continue to receive huge sums of money for doing absolutely nothing. Had thousands of years of civilisation come to this? Was there really no alternative? Jennifer decided, there and then, that there was.

'Piss off!' she shouted. And left.

Chapter 7 – The Man of God

'Ah dear boy, tell me what is troubling you?' the Bishop had said in his best benevolent voice. The Bishop saved his "dear boy" patter for spiritual crises. He'd seen a few in his time. He knew the score.

Sitting before him, head bowed and looking utterly defeated, was the Reverend Simon Halliday. Simon, who at 73 was actually a couple of years older than the Bishop, cast his eyes heavenward. 'I can't go on,' he said.

'I understand, my son. I understand.'

'No you don't,' Simon jabbered

'Yes I do. God sends us these challenges. The way of the cross is never easy.'

'But this is different.'

'Believe me, I know that it will feel different to you, my child. But these things are quite common.'

'I lost my faith in God thirty years ago,' said Simon, trying to shock some sense into the idiot sitting in the buttoned leather armchair opposite.

'God never lost faith in you.'

Simon's voice went up. 'Will you listen to me for one minute?'

'I am listening. God is listening.'

'My problem isn't that I've lost God. My problem is that I've found God.'

The Bishop's face fell. This was a new one. 'And the problem is?'

'The problem, Bishop, is that I've lost my faith.'

'But you just said that you've found God.'

'I had no faith in God.'

'What did you have faith in?'

'Capitalism.'

'You've lost your faith in capitalism?'

Simon nodded bleakly. 'It's awful. Everything I ever believed in has gone up in smoke.'

It was true. Things had never been the same for the Vicar since the Lehmann Brothers crash.

There he was in richest Surrey, pottering along with the Church of England and the global economy. Then bang! Everything changed. As markets tanked, the Reverend Simon Halliday mused upon mortgage-backed securities, the efficacies of the triple 'A' rating system - and the regrettable fact that so many allegedly intelligent people had fallen for what has quite obviously (to him) a Ponzi scheme. As a believer in the Austrian school of "creative destruction" Simon looked forward to the new and vibrant economy that would be born out of the ashes of the old. In between times, alas, it didn't look like much of the old economy would be robust enough to survive. A great many people would, for some years, experience a great deal of pain. Still, this was the natural way of things. Bankrupted fools had to lose their jobs. They were, self-evidently, unfit to do those jobs. You couldn't argue with capitalism.

Then they did start arguing with capitalism.

Hank Paulsen rolled out the TARP – the Troubled Asset Relief Programme. The what? Simon had never seen TARP mentioned by Adam Smith, the ancient Scottish inventor of economics, whose gory spectre was regularly invoked by the high priests of finance. This was just the start. Simon's entire belief system was brought crashing down by four words.

Too Big To Fail

The global economy, the entire shooting match, was a scam. It wasn't capitalism. There never was capitalism. There never would be capitalism.

The mere notion of capitalism only served as a front. Idiots were bailing out other idiots – in full view of a whole load of idiots who were letting them get away with it. Meanwhile, other idiots were attempting to create an intellectual construct to justify the idiocy. And everyone was walking around acting like this was the natural order of things.

It was then that the Reverend Simon Halliday realised that every physical thing around him was based on a lie. Every human interaction was being made under false pretences. People were living and dying a mirage. The only true thing was love. The only real thing was your soul. The only Universal was God.

'Oh don't spout that nonsense at me,' pleaded the Bishop. 'You're my top financial performer. What am I going to do without you?'

'I can't go on - financially. Spiritually, I'm reborn and ready to minister to the needs of the parish.'

The Bishop's face darkened. He knew Simon's parish well. The last thing it needed was spirituality.

'Faith in God is not incompatible with faith in our financial system,' the Bishop smiled.

'It is for me. Once belief has gone, you realise that the whole rancid system is only about fleecing the gullible.'

'We are all seeking a more equitable distribution of God's bounty,' said the Bishop, who wanted his own bounty to keep rolling in.

'At least my faith, my true faith, has returned.'

'For which God and I shall be eternally grateful.' The Bishop spoke between clenched teeth. 'I take it that you lost everything in the crash?'

'Oh no, I moved into cash and bonds, shorted the banks and made rather a lot.'

Simon handed over a cheque. The Bishop's eyes widened. He was used to receiving six figure cheques from Simon, but this was very nearly seven.

'Are you sure you can't be persuaded to keep speculating?'

'Absolutely not.'

'God has given you this talent for a reason.'

Simon managed a smile. 'Stay in cash, Bishop. It's my final word.'

The Bishop took on the look of a man who had made a decision. He stood up and guided Simon out.

'Clearly you need a fresh start somewhere else. My friend the Bishop of Winchester has the perfect parish for your new talents. It's called Foxhole Down. And it's idyllic.'

Simon knew then that he was in trouble. The Bishop hated the Bishop of Winchester. He was being sent to Foxhole Down to die with the parish.

*

Simon had packed a small case and walked the 115 miles to his Calvary. He slept in hedgerows, feeling too estranged from his own church to seek sanctuary in any of the vicarages on the way.

He remembered his first sight of the village. In the cool of dawn, he scrambled up to the top of the ridge. He had a twig in his hair and mud on his cheek. The village was bathed in golden light. His church, the highest building to be seen, nestled in to the side of the green. Here he would meet his last end.

Simon Halliday found himself smiling. He was at peace. Foxhole Down was going to be a wonderful place to pass away.

He scrambled down the slope, his bible thumping in his case. He was quite a sight, the most unlikely salesman that the village would ever see.

When he burst in to the church, Mrs Hugget was mopping the floor. She took one look at him, let out a shriek and ran for her life. Simon never saw her again. He had to do his own housekeeping, so he abandoned the flat and lived in a small room off the vestry. It was the perfect ascetic life for a 73 year-old widower.

Apart from the real bible, Simon's other bible had been the Financial Times. It was the only newspaper that bothered its arse with writing anything that remotely resembled the truth. Putting the nutty opinion pieces to one side, you could actually find out what was really going on. There was no point in reading it any longer. The writing was on the wall. The end was nigh.

Simon started off with six people in the congregation at his first service. After a month there were two – and they were both as deaf as posts. It didn't matter. As he saw it, evangelism had corrupted the church. There was no point in the spiritual reaching out to the temporal. Faith wasn't for sale. People either had it or they didn't. They were spiritual beings whether they acknowledged it or not. If he was to have a congregation, then it would find him.

Having resigned himself to death, Simon hadn't imagined living very long, although now he found life to be quite easy. He thought that he would wear himself down through malnourishment and let his heart give out.

But then things started to arrive.

It was practical things at first: a small table; a chair; a couple of cooking rings; a gas bottle; a cot to sleep in; some bedding. Then it was food: milk, bread, cereal; soups of all sorts; delicious stews. There was sometimes takeaway food too. Clothes came also, stout shirts and sturdy underwear. A laundry basket appeared. Then someone started to do his laundry. It was all very touching.

The Reverend Simon Halliday and the village were having a communion.

But no one came near his services. His sermons had been reported as being "odd" – even by their deaf listeners. Religion in the village, for the main part, was out. It was unneeded. It was unfashionable. There were doubts whether the Vicar could even be trusted with a funeral. There was likely to be an incident. The whole point of funerals was not to make too great a fuss over things. As Foxhole Down's sole representative of God and nothing else, its Vicar had unwittingly become its hermit.

The church door was open. Leaves were tumbling inside. Anouska liked this union of the holy world with the natural one. It reaffirmed the belief that she shared with the tribes of North America that the spirit world inhabited everything. She stood to let her eyes adjust to the dark light inside. Only stone and lead and glass, both stained and clear, could create such dim beauty. The acoustics of the building were perfect too. The sound of the wind, both in the trees outside and coming through the door, created a whispering choir of Aeolian beauty. Anouska checked. The door had been stoppered to a precise point. The sound was created by design. It was sensual perfection.

Seeing Simon on a kneeler in front of the altar, a thought popped into Anouska's head: he has all this to himself; he's the richest man alive.

The sound of the heels of her boots on the stones stirred the man from his prayer.

'Pull up a pew,' he said.

Anouska sat at the front, her legs extended, her feet crossed, her hands in the pocket of her coat. Simon sat beside her in an open white shirt, looking like a man just in from the fields. They had an excellent view of Saint George slaying his dragon.

'Let us pray,' he began.

'Pray for what?'

'Forgiveness.'

'Forgiveness for what?'

'For your entire career.'

'I take it that you're not a fan of modern art, Vicar.'

'I'm not a fan of anything to do with your imagination. Your entire being is a disgrace.'

'Just because I'm a rule breaker..'

'You don't break rules, you make it up as you go along.'

'I've thought very deeply about every aspect of my life and work. I resent your rancid male opinion. You, Reverend, are a misogynist.'

'Don't flatter yourself. I hate all human beings.'

They sat for a moment in mutual curmudgeonly silence. Their meetings always began with an argument.

'Why don't you do religious art?' said the Vicar.

'All art is religious art,' replied the artist.

'And all buildings are temples,' said Simon, looking around at his own.

'There's a new temple being erected on the green.'

'Mosque or synagogue?'

'A structure will be erected to the glorification of money.'

'Taller than the church?'

'It'll overshadow everything.'

'There's nothing like having the enemy right on your doorstep.'

'It'll be noisy too.'

'A noisy temple?'

'Money swears. Twenty-four hours a day.'

'Here I was, expecting to peg out quietly. I guess God has other ideas. What kind of temple is it?'

'It's one of big business's other ideas. An oil rig. With a derrick Foxhole Down is to be fracked.'

'The entire planet is to be fracked,' said Simon, resignedly. 'Humanity is fracked. Whatever you do, don't invest in it.'

'What do you know about investment?'

'Between 1980 and the year 2010 I gave my family an average annualized return of 14% year-on-year on the family inheritance. I got out of NASDAQ two weeks before the tech bubble burst. Switched everything into cash, gold and bonds because I saw the whole shadow banking, derivatives, Lehmann Brothers thing coming. They called me the "baby Buffett".' Simon's head dropped. 'Then I lost my faith.'

Anouska extended a consoling hand.

'I know all about fracking,' Simon brightened. 'It's a Ponzi scheme, funded in the US by hot money from the Federal Reserve. The big players got out at the beginning, leaving the suckers to suffer the shakedown.'

'But I thought it had transformed the American energy landscape?'

'It has. Briefly. It's just that investors don't know yet just how much they're going to lose. Production drops off a cliff after a couple of years.'

'Is it safe?'

'There's nothing that human beings do that is safe. If it's very tightly monitored and very tightly regulated, then the risks can be minimized. Unfortunately, our legislature is clueless.'

'What can we do?'

'Pray.'

'You pray. I'll paint,' Anouska stared blankly at her vicar. 'What can the rest of us do?'

'Britain's been stitched up so that there's nothing we can do.'

'You sound like Grassy Knoll.'

'"Conspiracy theorist" is the name you give to an enemy who is armed with the facts. We're going to have to play a highly devious game.'

Anouska smiled. Simon had just spoken one of her favourite words. She could see something stirring in the man of the cloth.

And it was stirring something in herself. He was tantalizingly unavailable. He was principled. He had an earthy and sensual spirituality. She would never attempt something so crass as to seduce him. If only he had been twenty years younger. She decided that she'd let him turn her into a thief; she'd steal glances at his soft blue eyes.

There was a pleasant tension between them. Simon's sexuality hadn't been extinguished. He had a few canvasses left in him.

'What's the goal?' he asked.

'We need to stop this.'

'All avenues of legitimate protest have been systematically removed. We'll only stop this by throwing ourselves under the wheels of their vehicles. And dying.'

'We have to die to protest?'

'Welcome to 21st century Britain.'

'There must be another way.'

'There is,' he said. 'I know someone who has explosives.'

Chapter 8 – The Fixer

Alan was normally awoken by birdsong. That morning, it was the gruff noise of large diesel engines that terminated his slumber.

He opened his curtains to an apocalyptic sight.

'Earth movers!' he shrieked. 'God protect us!'

The low loaders carrying the diggers were already on the green, their tyres chewing his beloved turf. They were on the wickets! Alan couldn't decide whether or not to shower before he dressed. His hands were shaking so much that he couldn't undo the bow on his pyjama trousers. This was no time for knots. It was no time for decorum either. He jumped into his wellington boots, put on his mackintosh and scrambled outside.

'Stop this madness!' he yelled.

'Want a bacon roll?' said a friendly Scottish voice.

Sitting on the small wall that surrounded Alan's front garden, eating a bacon roll, was a man who looked a bit like a Scottie dog.

'Get off my wall!'

'It's not your wall,' said the Scotsman offering a brown paper bag filled with bacon rolls. 'All property is theft. Karl Max said so.'

'Who, in God's name, are you?'

'I'm Hamish,' said Hamish.

'And what do you do?'

'I'm the Fixer.'

'You must stop this at once, it's illegal.'

'Me sitting on your wall – now that's illegal. This,' Hamish gestured at the enormous metal vehicles, 'is perfectly legal.'

'I order you to stop. I'm going to get a legal injunction.'

'Good luck with that,' said Hamish mockingly. 'If you've got any questions, talk to them.' He pointed at a police car. 'I fixed that too.'

Hamish was talking with his mouth full. It was very rude.

Alan looked at the squad car. There were two policemen sitting inside. They were also eating bacon rolls.

'You're going to need much more than two policemen,' said Alan defiantly.

'We've got as many policemen as it takes,' said the Fixer, 'and some of them could be wearing rather fetching riot gear. Are you planning to attack us in your pyjamas and wellington boots?'

Alan stood, feeling ridiculous.

'Foxhole Down!' Hamish used his most mocking voice again. He looked around the quaint and sleepy village. 'Not exactly a hotbed of protest.'

'But we've got money,' said Alan. 'And clout.'

'Obviously not enough,' said Hamish, watching the digger scoop up twenty yards of turf. 'Know anyone who's looking for a few thousand tonnes of topsoil?'

'Why are you doing this?'

'We need to prepare the ground for the heavy machinery that's coming. We'll put some gravel down. Then you'll see the drilling package arrive. It's quite a sight. A technically-minded man like you will enjoy it.'

'I won't enjoy anything! You're ruining the entire world!' Alan was becoming tearful. 'Who is behind this?'

'Zapata Drilling.'

'Who's that?'

'The Bush family. You know, from Texas? Well, they're originally from Massachusetts. You know the Bushes? Forty-first and forty-third Presidents of the United States? It's them. Although I think John Major's involved. And there's some Thatcher money too. You don't stand in the way of people like that. Not even in Foxhole Down. No matter how much money you've got. Or clout. I mean, you're going to have to have some big cahones if you're going to take that lot on. Those people are the definition of clout. They say Bill Clinton's going to come down and visit the site.'

'I thought the Bushes and Clintons were enemies?'

'That's just for the cameras. Slick Willie's up to his balls in oil. They all are. The old spinster next door better watch out when Clinton bowls up. He'll have her knickers off in no time. Not that she'll complain. She's gagging for it.'

The younger Alan would have thought about punching Hamish. The old Alan thrust his chin out and put on his most indignant voice.

'Jennifer is not gagging for anything!'

*

Jennifer was thinking about sex night and day. That horrid man had stirred something in her. He'd caused sex to rear its ugly head and now it couldn't be put back in its cage. The only thing was, sex's head wasn't ugly at all. It was something else altogether. It was wild and wanton and free. To be perfectly honest, Jennifer imagined that sex's head was a bit like Anouska's. It was a magnificent beast. Untameable. Animal desires had been awoken in Jennifer. She was going to make sure that they were satisfied. She'd bought lingerie. And she'd organised a makeover in Basingstoke.

She was convinced that this fracking disaster was going to provide lots of sexual opportunities.

Things were already looking up. Jennifer's first-ever love letter had dropped onto her doormat that very morning.

Dearest Lady on the Green, I'm still smarting from the skelping. You know how to hurt a man. I hope that your wrist is hurting too, so that you have physical memory of me. I can't stop thinking about you and the wild flash of passion in your eyes as you struck home. I deserved it. I am a bad man. I say bad things. I do bad things. My morals know no bounds. Looking for a bordello in Foxhole Down now seems like such a stupid thing to do. I have been too used to third world countries and I have forgotten the value of human life, especially of the feminine type. I have used many women over the years to satisfy my lusts. I am not proud, but I am not ashamed either. I got what I wanted and so did the girls. I know that we will never be a couple. I have ruined any chance of that. I am writing this letter to apologise for my crass words. I think your beauty took me by surprise. I am sorry for the emotional pain that my words may have caused. I am also sorry for the stooshie we are causing with the drilling. We will be gone in a couple of months, I promise. I want you to know that you are desirable. I desire you. We will see each other quite a lot. It would be better if we didn't mention our altercation. Feel free to slap me again. And again. And again. I'll apologise in advance for staring at you. I can't help myself. Warm regards, Hamish x

PS – Something is heading your way which will soften the blow of all the disruption.

Okay, he wasn't exactly Jane Austen, but Jennifer had read the letter ten times. The important thing was that she held sexual power over a man. And that felt fabulous. Looking from her window, she could see him sitting on Alan's wall. It looked like he was eating a bacon roll. He looked rough and coarse and dog-eared. He looked like exactly the kind of man she'd hate. Jennifer couldn't help thinking that she'd love to fight with him some more, rip his clothes off and tumble into bed for tumultuous sex. Sex, sometimes, was best with people you hated, she imagined.

She came away from the window, and turned her attention back to her muesli and natural yoghurt. Did she really want to sleep with the enemy? There would be lots of rough rig men in the weeks ahead. But others would come too: protesters; environmentalists; lovers of rural beauty. Someone heroic would perhaps come to her rescue. She was much better waiting for a courageous, handsome, outdoorsy environmental type with a good education and a bit behind him.

In the meantime, Jennifer re-read the letter and went back to the window to take another look at the forbidden fruit. It was then that she witnessed an act of betrayal which shocked her to the core.

The Major was selling bacon rolls to the truck drivers.

Chapter 9 Upside Down

St. Francis of Assisi Drilling Fluids' HQ was situated in a leafy suburb of Great Yarmouth. It wasn't what Jamie expected. Jamie had expected a sizeable office building attached to a warehouse full of chemicals. And some enormous storage tanks.

This was a pokey office in a converted space above a garage.

'Mind your head,' said Chris "Simmo" Simmonds, the CEO, Director and sole employee of St. Francis of Assisi Drilling Fluids.

Jamie cracked his head off the roof beam anyway. He collapsed into the only chair the office could accommodate. He could only sit upright by sticking his head into the skylight.

'Whereabouts in Spain do you live?'

'Oh, here and there,' said Jamie.

A sly smile crossed Simmo's face. 'And you're pretty new to the game?'

'One trip. For Fabian Drilling Fluids.'

'Just the one trip? What happened?'

'I didn't think they were a particularly professional outfit. I had no support from my colleague on the day shift.'

'Sadly, that's a common problem. Especially with drilling fluids. Lots of lazy engineers out there. We wouldn't touch them with a barge pole.'

'Glad to hear it,' said Jamie.

'Still,' said Simmo, 'you can count yourself lucky. I heard about some poor guy who went to a rig and the Toolpusher got murdered. And then he somehow managed to add several tonnes of cocaine to the drilling fluid. And he's gone on the run from Russian gangsters.'

'I met that guy!' yelled Jamie in faux-astonishment. 'We trained together.'

'What kind of training did you have?'

'It was three weeks. A couple of hours mixing mud in the lab. And then the rest of the day was a technical Q & A session. In the pub. It was a lying, shagged-out old engineer called Bert.'

'Bert's still alive?' Simmo was genuinely shocked. 'I thought he'd have drunk himself to death by now. He's trained half the mud engineers in the North Sea. Did he mention me?'

'Yes,' Jamie lied.

'I bet it wasn't good.'

'Horrendous.'

'I don't know what it is with some people,' Simmo sighed. 'Every time they move their lips, lies come out.'

'That's why it's such a refreshing change to deal with someone as straightforward as yourself,' said Jamie faux-earnestly.

'I think we're on the same wavelength,' Simmo smiled. 'You're just the kind of engineer we need.'

'So I'm hired?'

'How does four hundred a day sound?'

'Sounds like a deal.'

They shook hands.

'I assume that I'll be working on night shift,' said Jamie. 'Given that I'm still pretty green, I hope the engineer on day shift will be experienced and co-operative.'

Simmo leaned back in his chair and beamed a radiant smile at Jamie. 'You'll love the engineer on day shift.'

Antonia was waiting outside in a car.

She kissed him. 'How did it go?'

'We're working together on the Hampshire job. But I think he's going to lumber me with a dodgy guy on day shift. There's something topsy-turvy about this entire enterprise.'

*

There was a crisis meeting in the Royal Oak. Alan arrived. In a state. In his pyjamas. He was immediately given a pint of champagne. He dribbled half of it down his chin. Grassy Knoll was already having a pint of real ale. It was half past nine in the morning.

Jennifer stormed in. 'Jezebel!' she screamed at the Major.

'I think you'll find that I'm a Judas, old girl,' the Major replied. 'Let's not confuse our biblical characters.'

'Don't you condescend to me. I've slapped once and I'll slap again. I know perfectly well what you are. And it is a Jezebel. Whore!'

'What's happened?' Grassy Knoll wiped the froth from his top lip.

'This!' Jennifer pointed at the Major. 'De-commissioned invertebrate! Has been selling bacon rolls to the enemy.'

'It seemed rude not to,' said the Major. 'I had rolls and bacon in the freezer. The men asked. They reminded me of the squaddies I'd fought alongside. Salt of the earth. This isn't their doing. They're just the workers.'

'How much did you charge?' said Grassy Knoll.

'Three quid a roll.'

'Well done, Major,' said Grassy Knoll. 'Never miss an opportunity to exploit the working classes.'

'That's great coming from you,' said Jennifer. 'Remind me, what is it you do for a living?'

'US bonds and the US dollar are doing very nicely for me at the moment.'

'You're hardly Che Guevara.'

'Hark at Emily Pankhurst,' said Grassy Knoll acidly.

'They've dug up my life's work,' said Alan in a weak and woeful voice. 'In seconds.'

'Drink, Jennifer?' said the Major.

'I certainly do not want a drink from you. I've a good mind to have you reported and this place closed down.'

'Oh God,' said Grassy Knoll. 'As if things aren't bad enough.'

'Close me down if you like,' said the Major. 'I'll convert the place to apartments and be done with you all.'

'It hasn't taken long for us to start fighting among ourselves.'

It was Anouska. She had arrived. Jennifer wondered how the woman managed to look so perfect so early in the morning. She was top-to-toe in Prada with a Ferragamo handbag, not that Jennifer would have known.

'The Major is selling bacon rolls to the enemy,' said Jennifer tartly.

'Good for him,' said Anouska. 'We need to build bridges. All the better to blow them to smithereens later. We have to think tactically, ladies and gentlemen.'

'Tactically, Major,' said Jennifer pointedly. 'Not profitably.'

Anouska continued. 'It hasn't taken them long to break turf. These bastards don't mess about. Rust never sleeps.'

'You're the one with money, Anouska!' Alan shouted. 'Do something! We have to stop them before it's too late! Take an injunction out!'

'What do you think I've been doing all morning?'

'Hair and make-up?' offered Jennifer.

'Aaaarh!' Anouska let out a shriek of frustration. 'Give me a pint, Major.'

'Beer or champagne?'

'Vodka,' said Anouska sarcastically, glaring at Jennifer, who lowered her eyes. 'What's the ridiculously-named cask ale called? Sneck Pecker? Sheep Tupper?'

'Upside Down.'

'Sounds about right.'

'One pint of Upside Down. Coming up.'

'And very quickly going down,' said Anouska, lighting a Gauloise.

'You can't smoke in here!'

'Fuck off Jennifer,' said Anouska. 'The world is ending. Or hadn't you noticed?'

A shadow fell on the company as a large dump truck drove past, filled with soil.

'The good news is that I've got a big-swinging-dick City barrister working on the case. That's what you like, isn't it, Jennifer? Big swinging dicks?' Anouska exhaled a satisfying plume of smoke. 'He's right up your street: Basil Cuthbert QC.'

Jennifer reddened. The Major handed a pint over to Anouska and raised an eyebrow.

'Oh come here,' Anouska drew Jennifer to her in a hug. She whispered in her ear. 'Don't take me so seriously. Don't take life so seriously.'

Anouska kissed Jennifer's cheek tenderly, and erotically.

Jennifer's face turned from red to puce.

'There will be no injunction,' Anouska continued. It appears that the forces of darkness have that end of things stitched up. It's been through parliament and the House of Lords.'

'But we have rights,' said Alan.

'You had rights,' Anouska replied. 'The legislation is watertight. They can drill and frack under anyone's house.'

'But they can't create a racket on the green with houses surrounding it? Can they?'

'One of the best legal minds in Britain is checking that out right now. But he's not hopeful.'

'You've been legislatively ambushed,' said a Scottish voice.

All heads turned. Hamish had entered the building.

'You've got no chance. The tanks were quietly moved into position while you lot were watching your house prices go up. You're fucked. Pint of Upside Down, please.'

'Don't serve him!' said Jennifer.

The Major began to pull a pint.

'Bacon rolls are one thing, but alcohol…'

'Let's hear what the lad has to say,' said the Major. 'The hospitality provided by this tavern is an ancient and honourable thing that stretches back for centuries…'

'Until you ended it abruptly at eight o'clock this morning dishing bacon rolls out to the very people intent on destroying our ancient way of life,' said Jennifer.

The company took a moment to muse silently upon whether watching ballroom dancing on the BBC and shopping for pre-packaged beetroot in out-of-town superstores constituted an ancient way of life.

'Och, calm yourself,' said Hamish. 'We're the most exciting thing that's come to this village since the Black Death.'

'We survived the Black Death, and we'll survive you,' said Jennifer.

'That's the spirit!' said Hamish. 'In six months' time, it'll be as if we were never here. Almost,' he added softly, staring at Jennifer.

'Who are you?' said Anouska.

'I'm Hamish McGee.'

'And what do you do?'

'I'm the Fixer.'

'What do you fix?'

'I fix whatever needs to be done to make things happen. In a drilling sense. I smooth things over.'

'You bribe people,' said Grassy Knoll.

'Grassy Knoll, I presume,' said Hamish, extending a hand.

Grassy Knoll shook hands tentatively and smiled a little, pleased that his reputation had preceded him.

'You won't bribe any of the people around here,' said Alan defiantly.

'I wouldn't dream of it,' said Hamish. 'Things are so much easier to organise here. The British government is incredibly co-operative.'

'They were bought and paid for,' said Grassy Knoll, 'years ago.'

'I wouldn't know anything about that,' said Hamish. 'That's fixed by a bigger league of fixers.'

'You're more used to pushing tribespeople around,' said Jennifer.

'I've met some lovely tribes,' said Hamish, with a wink.

Hamish cast his eyes over this peculiar tribe: Alan, in pyjamas, wellies and raincoat, the village elder; Jennifer, who had never quite gotten on top of how to apply the war paint; Grassy Knoll, a warrior whose weapons were all in his mind; Anouska, the chief and true warrior, majestic in perfect war paint and dressed to kill; and the Major, leaning on an ale pump, Foxhole Down's version of a medicine man.

A sharp blast of icy wind brought another person into the company.

'Sweet Jesus,' said Hamish, 'it's the village shaman.'

The Vicar had arrived. With twigs in his hair. Leaves in his shirt. And soil on his suit.

'I've just lobbed a couple of mud balls at your men,' he said gently. 'I hope you don't mind. Felt like the right thing to do. Not very Christian, I'm afraid.'

'Christ in the temple,' said Anouska. 'With the money lenders. His finest moment.'

'My house shall be called the house of prayer; but ye have made it a den of thieves.' The Vicar looked upon Hamish with kindness, warmth and love. It was a withering look.

'Let he who is without sin cast the first stone,' said Hamish eventually, recovering himself. 'Is there anyone here who hasn't used hydrocarbons?'

There was silence amongst the tribe.

'Oil has to come from somewhere,' Hamish continued. 'And now that we're getting desperate, it has to come from here. I've been in worse shit-holes.'

'That's what you do. Turn everywhere into a shit-hole,' said Anouska. 'And that is why you have the fight of your life on your hands.'

'You get your lawyers. We'll get ours. You might as well protest against the steam engine.'

'You represent the technology of death,' said the Vicar. 'People will choose life.'

'I know what people will choose,' said Hamish, 'which is why I am delighted to announce that there will be a windfall bonus of one thousand pounds per household.'

'A bribe,' said Alan. 'What did I tell you?'

'I think you'll find the people of this village will be only too happy to receive it.'

There was another shock of cold air. A tough-looking man had come in. He had a thick Hampshire accent.

'Yes or no, Major? Yes or no?'

'No Fletcher. I'm not serving you, or any of your family.'

'Serving beer out of hours? I'd watch that if I were you,' said Fletcher. He left.

'He'll take your thousand pounds,' said Alan.

'He'll take two thousand pounds,' said Jennifer. 'The Fletchers live in two houses knocked into one.'

'They've been here forever,' said Grassy Knoll, anticipating Hamish's questions. 'Been causing trouble forever. No one likes them.'

Hamish grinned. 'If you don't like the Fletchers, wait until you meet the drillcrew.'

Chapter 10 - It's Just Not Cricket

Things moved quickly. No sooner had the green's turf and topsoil been removed, than another set of trucks, bearing aggregate, arrived. The bladed earthmovers, which had sliced the cricket pitch apart, now smoothed the stones into place, to provide a site fit for heavy equipment. A small security booth was set up, with a man in a dark jumper coordinating movements. Sales of bacon rolls were brisk.

Then one day the drilling package arrived.

It came on trucks with a police escort. It was all flashing lights and "Wide Load" signs. It came from Germany. Its transit slowed the motorways that the convoy was on. It created major problems on the trunk roads. It completely snarled up the country lanes around Foxhole Down.

There was only one road in and out of the village. The east road was backed up with trucks waiting to unload. Access and egress for other traffic was by the west road, which meant a twenty mile detour for people going in the wrong direction. The man in the dark jumper had a stressful time.

It all bolted together, like some nightmare flat-pack piece of furniture. Wheels were jacked up. Pistons were extended. Blocks of wood were used where appropriate. A fifty tonne crane lifted everything into position. It was all very clever.

Alan positioned a chair in his front room, to get a good view of things. He appreciated the cleverness. He could even perceive some beauty. Artists like Anouska thought that beauty was all about looks. They couldn't appreciate that beauty could also derive from functionality. Alan understood this. After all, he had made things. There was some beauty to behold – if you understood what you were looking at. The ghastly reality was the context in which it was all happening.

Alan knew that to make an omelette you had to break a few eggs. This was the wrong omelette. In the wrong place. With the wrong eggs.

It was all Alan could do to stop from weeping. He could never have foreseen his life ending like this. It was bad enough that there was no cricket on the green. Never in his worst nightmares could he have imagined that there would be no green to have cricket on.

In all, it took three days to put together. When it was complete, Alan stood outside the house of his father, grandfather and great-grandfather. In the gloaming's dying light, he saw that the derrick was standing right where the wicket-keeper used to. The drillfloor covered the slip area, on both the on-side and the leg-side. A set of open-topped tanks stretched from square leg to mid-wicket. A flight of stairs descended to backward point. There were cabins and offices at long-off and long-on, drillpipe racks at deep cover and portable toilets at deep backward square leg. The generators were, thankfully, at third man, although the villagers on the opposite side of the green wouldn't be so thankful for that. There were containers and sealed tanks between fine leg and long leg, more cabins, offices and changing rooms around deep mid-wicket and a car park at deep extra cover.

At silly mid-off, where the silliest, and bravest, fielder stood, where Alan had stood the best years of his life, was a large drill bit. What a silly place to put a silly thing, Alan thought. The bit would soon be scarring the landscape forever, creating a hole down which they would force all kinds of poisons. God alone knew where they would end up. Very silly. And other kinds of toxins would come back out, to make profits for god-knows who. All too silly. There would be leaks and spills, as there always were. Bungles and apologies and cover-ups. Silly, silly silly. It was a silly life in a silly economy and Alan, he realised, was a silly old man living out a silly old life, who thought that the world owed him a quiet end in a tranquil and unspoilt corner of the earth that would be forever England.

'What the hell has happened here?' said a Scottish voice.

Standing in front of Alan was a lanky, dark-haired man in his late twenties with a deep suntan.

'Are you drilling chaps all Scottish?'

'I couldn't say,' said the Scot. 'I'd assume there will be some English guys. The logger's Spanish.'

'A logger? You're going to cut the trees down?' Alan felt his legs going.

'No, we're not going to cut anything down!' said the Scot, as he steadied Alan. 'She'll be logging data, not trees. I'm Jamie, by the way.'

'"Thank-you, young man,' said Alan, standing alone again.

Jamie let out a long whistle. 'What a catastrophe. I had no idea they would do this on a village green.' Jamie suddenly spotted something he hadn't expected. 'My goodness, is that a cricket pavilion?'

'Yes,' Alan's voice cracked.

Jamie looked at Alan in disbelief. 'And you've let them do this?'

'We couldn't stop them. We've been stitched up. By Parliament.'

'I'll say you have,' said Jamie. 'And here was me thinking that an Englishman's home was his castle.'

'They've shredded the Magna Carta while our house prices have been going up,' said Alan, his voice steadying. He was beginning to realise that, for the moment, anger was his best emotional friend.

'I can't imagine this doing much for the local housing market,' said Jamie ruefully. 'I feel as if I should apologise, but I'm just one of the workers. In the grand scheme of things, I'm nothing.'

'That's what this has taught me,' said Alan. 'In the grand scheme of things, we're all nothing.'

'Tell me about it,' said Jamie, ruefully.

'Are you the mud engineer?' shouted Hamish.

'One of them,' Jamie replied.

'There's two?' Hamish approached to get a closer look at Jamie.

'Me and another guy on day shift,' said Jamie.

'Aye, right,' laughed Hamish. 'Don't tell me you've fallen for that one.'

'What one?'

'Telling someone that they're working a twelve hour shift, when they're really providing twenty-four hour cover. It's the oldest con in the oilfield.'

The colour drained from Jamie's face.

'How many years' experience have you got?'

'Ten,' Jamie lied.

Hamish turned to Alan. 'Do you believe him?'

'Not a chance,' said Alan.

'Everyone in the oil business is a liar. But at least tell us some credible fibs.'

A mud ball exploded against the fence behind them.

'Afternoon Vicar,' Hamish waved.

'God be with you,' the Vicar waved back.

Hamish turned back to Alan. 'Do you think he's likely to escalate his violence?'

'Anything's possible. They sent him here to die.'

Hamish turned back to Jamie. 'How many years' experience did you say you have?'

'Three.'

'That's a bit more like it. The Rooster's going to love you.'

'The last time someone said something like that to me, things didn't work out so well.'

'Didn't work out for who?'

'For anyone,' said Jamie. 'Who's the Rooster?'

'Rooster McGraw. The wickedest Client Rep in Christendom. There's only two legends in fracking – and Rooster McGraw is both of them.'

Chapter 11 - Accommodation

Hamish showed Jamie to his cabin.

'It's not plumbed-in, so there's no water. It's not wired in, so there's no electricity. Someone stole the TV aerial, so there's no TV signal, which is just as well, 'cos someone stole the TV too.'

The cabin was the most dismal abode Jamie had seen since he abided on an oil rig offshore. The entire place was filthy, not helped by Hamish's muddy boots tramping everywhere. There was a tiny bedroom barely containing a single bed, which had a mattress with some dubious stains on it. There was a tiny toilet, barely containing a toilet bowl, shower head and sink. There was a recess, trying to pass itself off as a kitchen, barely containing a cooker, a microwave and a fridge.

'Someone stole the pots,' said Hamish.

'There was a laboratory which had a few benches, a few drawers, a rusty cupboard, a window and a sink.

'Looks like the chair's gone missing too,' said Hamish.

'I wouldn't let an animal live like this,' said Alan.

'Welcome to the oilfield,' said Hamish. 'It's shit. And what are you doing here? You weren't supposed to follow us. You're trespassing.'

'Arrest me,' said Alan. 'The Vicar's not the only one with nothing to lose.'

'If we're going to get through this,' said Jamie, 'we're going to have to come to some kind of accommodation with the locals.'

'Talking of accommodation, you'll get a bed for the night at a reasonable rate at the Fletchers'. They're a lovely family.' Alan smiled.

'It might be an idea,' said Hamish, 'until we get this place fixed up. They're probably the only family in the village that will welcome us with open arms. Everyone says they're a top bunch.'

*

The minute Jamie was alone, he rang Simmo. Or tried to. There was no mobile signal in his cabin. There was no mobile signal on the site. And there was no mobile signal anywhere in the village. Jamie had to climb halfway up the hill before he got a couple of bars.

Before Simmo even said a word, Jamie could hear the familiar, friendly sound of a busy pub in the background.

'Simmo! It's Jamie! There's no lead engineer!'

'I know. I'm in London right now, trying to track the bugger down. He's gone on a bender. If I can find him and sober him up, he'll be with you the day after tomorrow. Until then, sit tight.'

'I can't do this on my own!'

'This isn't like offshore drilling, where they've got you prisoner.'

Jamie thought about his one and only trip to the North Sea. He had to admit, if the ability to run away to a pub had existed, there wouldn't have been any drillcrew left.

'Land jobs are tough,' Simmo continued. 'The guys that do it are all a bit cranky, especially mud engineers.'

Jamie thought about the mud engineers he had worked with. They were, to a man, completely barking mad.

'Okay,' Jamie said. 'My cabin's not ready. If I stay locally, will you reimburse me?'

'Make sure you get a receipt. The client will cover it. Charge for anything you like. These people are loaded. It's Surrey money. They've just sent me a whopping advance.'

Jamie could hear a woman giggling in the background. There was a crunching sound. And then Simmo giggled. It sounded like he was getting his ears licked.

'How much can I charge a night?'

'Use a guest house and get them to make the receipt out for two hundred quid. You and me can split the profit. Same with meals. Think like an MP. But don't charge for drink. They don't like it when you take the piss.'

Jamie lost his signal and the call ended. He stumbled down the hill in the dark and made for the pub. He suspected that the night ahead was best confronted with some alcohol in him.

Jamie didn't get very far before he stumbled over a decaying log and fell flat on his face. He smiled to himself. Falling down was normal for him. So long as you were able to get back up. This he did. An owl hooted. Then again, it could have been a wood pigeon. Jamie didn't have a clue.

What he was aware of was the fact that this wood appeared to have more life in it by night than it did during the day. It was an ancient wood and felt as old as the hill he was standing on. Nestled below was the village, twinkling warmly. Sitting snugly, it was a comforting sight and spoke to Jamie of hearth and home. One of the lights was from an old alehouse, serving warm foaming liquids and offering traditional hospitality. Jamie wondered what kind of reception he'd get there. For the moment, he was happy to be amongst the whispering trees.

Then the rig's floodlights were turned on, illuminating the green like a football stadium. It wasn't a pretty site. So much of modern technology was over-lit.

As quickly as they had come on, the lights went out. Magically, the village was returned to its cosy and enchanting self. World order properly restored, Jamie felt his way forward with his feet. He could almost hear the dying ferns part and the soft grass yielding under his feet. The occasional snap of a twig came as a delightful shock. Jamie was enjoying himself. But he soon became aware his feet weren't the only feet that were snapping twigs.

Then, like an Arapaho, out of nowhere, the Vicar suddenly appeared.

'Waaargh!' shrieked Jamie.

The Vicar was wearing a ghostly white cotton chemise.

'How did you sneak up on me like that?' Jamie asked.

'I live with nature. I don't blunder through it like an inept thief.'

'You should teach me.'

'You should stop stealing.'

'I'm not stealing.'

'Yes you are. What are you going to take out of the ground?'

'Oil, maybe gas.'

'And what are you going to put back?'

'Nothing. Well, maybe some chemicals. By the sound of things, a load of toxic chemicals.'

'You see,' said the Vicar, 'it doesn't work, does it?'

'No,' Jamie admitted, trying not to look crestfallen in the moonlight.

'We can't continue this way, can we?'

'Suppose not.' Jamie felt like he was seven years old.

'I'm going to convert you.' The lunar light glinted in the Vicar's sapphire blue eyes. The man was deadly serious.

'Why do you guys always have to convert people to God?'

'I'm not going to convert you to God, you idiot. God is self-evident. Jesus is self-evident. I'm going to convert you to Gaia.'

'Who's Gaia?'

The vicar pointed at his feet. 'Mother Earth.'

'What kind of vicar are you, Vicar?'

The Vicar let out a very unnerving laugh.

'I'm the head of The Dying Church of the Living World. I'm not here to save you from the Devil. I'm here to save you from yourself.'

Jamie edged away, down the hill. 'I appreciate the concern, Vicar. I really do. But things are very complicated in my life. And it's best I remain here.'

'We'll talk,' said the Vicar. 'My church is always open.'

Jamie looked back, but like an Arapaho, the Vicar was gone.

Chapter 12 – Thieves, Pimps & Arsonists

By the time that Jamie made it to the village, the wind had picked up. The sign of the Royal Oak was swinging and creaking. Jamie felt as if he was walking into the The Admiral Benbow Tavern in Treasure Island. It sounded like there were pirates inside. A new light had come on, to the left of the entrance. The Major had opened the snug.

Jamie turned right and went into the lounge.

'You look like one of the drilling mob,' said the Major.

'I was hoping that I resembled a human being,' replied Jamie politely.

'The rig types are in there.' The Major pointed to the snug.

'You make it sound like apartheid.'

'You're lucky I'm serving you at all. And I don't want any oil nonsense.'

Jamie had no idea what the Major meant by "oil nonsense". Then he thought about the shenanigans that had happened on his first trio offshore: the deaths, the love affairs, the randy roustabouts, the cocaine and the cribbage.

So there really was quite a lot of "oil nonsense". Jamie had a dreadful feeling that there would be a lot more.

'Will you do me a favour?' Jamie asked.

The Major made no reply.

'If you see or hear any Russians, let me know. I'll reward you handsomely.'

'No oil nonsense,' repeated the Major.

There were three men in the snug. It was a tall American with a languid southern drawl who spoke first.

'Looks like we got ourselves a mud man.'

Jamie smiled lamely. He hated being called a "mud man". He was a drilling fluids engineer, thank-you very much, even if they did call his fluid "mud".

'How many years' experience you got?'

'Three.'

Hamish was sitting next to the American. He said nothing.

'What's your name, boy?'

'Jamie Chivers.'

'Well you better go and get your passport, because I don't believe a fucking word that comes out of your mouth.'

'You're the second American who's said that to me.'

'The other guy was a genius too.' The American extended a massive hand. 'Rooster McGraw.'

Knowing what was coming was of no help to Jamie. He pumped Rooster's hand as fiercely as he could, but his own hand got crushed all the same.

'I'm the company man. The head honcho.' Rooster refused to let go. Jamie could have predicted this too. 'If you fuck up, come and tell me. I'll deal with it. Lie to me, and I'll crucify you. I'll personally hammer the nails in myself.'

Jamie twisted his hand free. 'Have you met the Vicar?' he asked.

'No, but I'm going to get him to bless the site.'

'He won't do it. He hates us.'

'You don't know how to talk to a preacher. I'll make him an offer he can't refuse. God comes from Louisiana. Everybody knows that. Major! If you please. This boy needs to go upside down.'

The Major poured a pint for Jamie – and three more for the others. Rooster handed over a fifty pound note. The Major gave back no change. A ritual had been established.

'The money is flowing like honey,' said Rooster. 'We have a great client. Here's to Surrey money, whatever the hell that is.'

The company raised their glasses.

'Let's all get rich!'

*

'Bastards,' said Anouska.

The natives could hear every word coming from the snug. They were having another pow-wow in the lounge.

'They think everything is about money,' said Alan.

'Turns out they're right,' said Grassy Knoll. 'I went round the village. I knocked on every door. All the incomers are happy to take the thousand pound bribe. Hamish had been there before me. I didn't get a single vote of support. Not one.'

'These new people are all dead,' said Alan. 'They want to live in a small community, but they don't understand what a small community is.'

'I'm disappointed in you,' said Anouska to the Major. 'It was bad enough that you sold them bacon rolls. Now you've got them snugly in the snug. What betrayal do you have in mind next?'

'It's fabulous. They've no catering. I'm going to do lunches for the day shift and a 10 pm delivery of soup and stew for the night shift.'

'You slimy, backstabbing…. fuck,' said Alan.

This brought silence. It was the first time that Alan had sworn in living memory.

'I'm shocked,' said Anouska. 'And I don't shock easily.'

'Well really,' said Alan, 'This is the bitter end.'

'It's my final payday,' said the Major, 'before I sell this off for flats. There's no viable business here. I don't even know what it is you're fighting for. The local shop died. The cricket club died. The church is dying. The pub is dying. All you care about is the view from your over-priced properties. There's nothing in this village left to save. The community died years ago.'

It was Jennifer who finally spoke up. 'I'll fight for my neighbours and I'll fight for this landscape and I'll fight for every living thing in it.'

'Hear hear,' said the others.

'There's four of you,' said the Major. 'Good luck.'

'We may be small in number,' said Anouska, 'but we're well-connected. The mother of all media storms is about to hit them.'

Anouska raised her voice and shouted through to the snug.

'You're not going to get rich! You're going to get attacked!'

*

Back in the snug, Jamie went to join the third man, sitting in the corner. He was a squat fellow, with close-shorn greyish dark hair. Dressed darkly, he looked like a mole. He spoke in confidential northern English tones.

'You the mud engineer? I'm Col, the derrickman.'

Jamie's blood chilled. The last derrickman he'd worked with was dead. Very very dead.

'I hope things work out well for you,' said Jamie.

'Why wouldn't they?' said Col, suspiciously.

'I mean I hope the job goes well! And we can work brilliantly together. I'll look after you. Let's cooperate. And liaise. And if anything goes wrong, I'll take the blame.'

'I hope you're more relaxed on the site than you are in a pub. I don't like mud engineers who flap.'

Colin's tone was downright sinister. What he said next didn't help.

'How many times have you been arrested?'

'Once,' Jamie lied.

'What for?'

'Murder.'

'Did you do it?'

'No, but I found out who did.'

'Who was it?'

'The derrickman.'

'And he's roaming around free?'

'No, he's roaming around dead.'

Col looked at Jamie with new respect.

'Keep that under your hat,' Jamie continued. 'What have you been arrested for?'

'Assault, mainly. I've got a charge of actual bodily harm coming up. Against me mate. I'm not a bad lad, I just get a bit silly with a pint in me.'

Col gulped his pint.

The door opened and the rest of the drill crew came in. Or tried to. The snug was too snug and besides, both shifts were working on dayshift to speed the construction of the rig. Things started to get a bit heated as more bodies were crammed in. There was a bit of pushing and shoving. Voices were raised. Rooster ordered everybody outside to sit on the sidewalk, while the Major ferried trays of lager and ale to the twenty men.

As they gathered outside, Jamie took a good look at the crew. They weren't an inspiring sight. The offshore crew that he had worked with before had, give or take a few additional moustaches, looked like a regular bunch of British guys. This mob looked like a regular bunch of thieves, pimps and arsonists.

Simmo was right. Land drilling was different.

Even Rooster was casting a wary eye over them. 'Where the hell is your Toolpusher?'

Jamie's blood ran a little cold once again. The last Toolpusher he had worked with was also very very dead.

'He's chasing the electrician through the woods,' said a squat Mexican, picking his golden teeth with a knife.

'Did the floodlights trip the generators or the generators trip the floodlights?' asked Rooster.

'That was the argument that started the fight.'

'What's your drilling company called?'

'Lohag Drilling,' said a fat pimp, his corpulent face poking out of an ankle-length pink fur coat.

'Like a low hag?'

'It's an acronym,' said a shifty-looking English arsonist. The full company name is "Land of Hope and Glory Drilling".'

'I'm guessin' that ain't a Texas outfit,' said Rooster.

'British Virgin Islands.'

'A tax front? No shit. I bet it was incorporated about three months ago.'

'Four.'

'This job gets better and better. And when the lights came on for thirty seconds, your unit looked like some refurbished crock-of-shit rig I worked on ten years ago in Azerbaijan.'

'The market for land rigs is tight, what with all this fracking drilling,' said a scheming pimp, who also looked like a bit of an arsonist.

'I hope the client has got deep pockets,' said Jamie.

'I hope the preacher has got double-strength Holy Water,' said Rooster.

'It'll take more than Holy Water to sort this crew out,' said Jamie.

It was at this point that the Toolpusher arrived. He was six foot two of mud, blood and bruises.

'Hey Beezer, looks like you got your ass kicked by the electrician,' said the lanky Latino.

'I didn't get my ass kicked by the electrician,' said Beezer defiantly. 'I got my ass kicked by the Vicar.'

'That man creeps through those woods like the God-damn Viet Cong,' said Rooster. 'And I should know.'

Jamie listened closely to the crew. He was relieved not to hear any Russian voices.

Rooster let out a loud whistle to silence the crew.

'Listen up!' he began. 'We all know that when God made salmon, he put them in the most beautiful places on earth. And when he made oil he put it in every single shit-hole known to man.'

This received a smattering of applause.

'Now it looks as if our luck has turned. This is the best shit-hole I've ever seen.'

'Amen!' shouted an American. Glasses were raised.

'But we can't treat this shit-hole like the others. We can't push these people around like the others. Folks here have got rights. More importantly, they've got connections. The natives here are as weird as shit. They've all got broomsticks up their rear ends. Any incident with a native will be treated as seriously as an incident on the job. And you'll get your sorry ass run off this site. The womenfolk are to be treated with respect. They're not whores like everywhere else.'

'Where's the whorehouse?' said the fat pimp.

'There's no whorehouse, I'm afraid,' said Hamish. 'And it gets worse. The women here are all respectable. There's not a slapper amongst them.'

There were shouts of disgust and derisory shrieks. Jamie could feel the mood turning nasty. A glass was thrown. It smashed at Rooster's cowboy-booted feet.

'Settle down!' Rooster bellowed. 'England is full of whores. Just not in this village. If you don't find them, they'll sure as hell find you.'

There was cheering. Another glass was thrown. It smashed at Jamie's feet. He moved to stand behind Rooster.

'So let's make some hole!' Rooster went on, to more cheers. 'Let's drill this bitch, log it, case it and frack the hell out of it. And don't think of quitting on the job. There's a bottom hole bonus of one hundred dollars per day per man. If you stay 'til the end of the well in thirty days that makes....'

'Three thousand dollars,' Jamie whispered.

'Three thousand dollars per man!' Rooster yelled, to more cheers. 'And there will be no knife fights neither. No shooting animals in the woods. No shooting traffic signs. And no shooting locals.'

'What about cutting them trees down?'

'We can't touch the trees,' said Rooster, sadly. 'But that pesky whatsit. That cricket pavilion thing. That's gonna meet with the wrong end of a crane. We'll flatten the bastard and use it for firewood.'

There was a cry of 'No!' And then a thud.

The locals had come out of the pub to listen. And Alan had just fainted. Two of the bewildered foursome tended to their fallen comrade.

'Don't you dare touch the cricket pavilion,' Anouska shouted. 'It's listed.'

Anouska, predictably, awoke the animal spirits in the crew. They whistled and cat-called.

'Hell will freeze over before I'd touch one of you,' she said derisively.

'And me neither,' said Jennifer emphatically.

The crew laughed.

'Hey gorgeous,' shouted the fat pimp to Anouska, 'you might not get the choice.'

There were more whistles. That was enough for Rooster. He waded into his crew and punched one of them at random. The crew then started punching each other at random.

Anouska had come prepared. She produced an empty champagne bottle and started biffing men over the head at random. It was like a violent game of rounders.

Jennifer hadn't come prepared. She got grabbed.

Jamie found himself being sucked into the brawl. He valiantly tried to calm things down. But as quickly as he could pull men apart, they set about one another again.

'Peace-making is utterly pointless,' he said to Anouska, who had pulled herself free and had lit a cigarette.

'Violence is so much fun,' said Anouska, coshing an unfortunate Jamaican, who was already on his knees. The poor guy sank to the ground and Anouska looked at the unbroken bottle with deep satisfaction. 'I always knew that there was a fundamentally sound reason for drinking champagne.'

Jamie looked out over the picturesque village, its ancient church, its modern oil rig and its embattled crew. He had a fundamentally strange feeling of a world gone badly awry.

A yelp alerted him to the fact that Jennifer was being dragged down. Anouska handed him the bottle and Jamie waded in. When he hit the thieving, pimping arsonist over the head, the bottle bounced out of his hand, sailed over everyone's head and shattered on the pub's steps.

'Stop! Stop!' Jamie yelled.

Amazingly, they did.

'We can't carry on like this,' Jamie said. 'This is Hampshire, for goodness sake. It's not the Third World.'

'It will be when we're finished with it,' said the fat, bruised pimp.

'The kid's right,' Rooster yelled. 'This is what drinking and drilling does. Anyone caught drinking on the job will get their sorry ass run off this job. As of tomorrow. Today, the drinks are on Rooster!'

As the crew headed toward the pub, the locals retreated, carrying their wounded with them.

The Major guided them, not into the lounge, but into the snug. The locals had been relegated. The drilling crew had taken over the pub.

Chapter 13 – Birds Instead of Saints

Fortified by four pints of Upside Down, Jamie toddled along the outside of the site's perimeter fence to the opposite end of the green from the church. He felt that this kind of drilling was vastly preferable to the offshore type. He had fallen in love with Foxhole Down. It was picture postcard perfect. He loved the trees on the green. He loved the ancient woodland that was all around. He loved the smooth rise of the down itself. The church was just everything that you could want from a pretty English village. The cottages around the green were quaint beyond belief. He adored the Ye Olde Pubbe with its undulating floors and skew-whiff walls. He felt that he was drinking in the footsteps of Dick Turpin and Robin Hood. The locally-made ale was a gently intoxicating revelation. Even the cranky locals were charming in their own way.

Jamie couldn't think of a better place to hide from Russians.

It was a pity about the drilling package and all that gravel and noise over the cricket pitch, but Jamie was convinced that it was perfectly safe. Otherwise, it wouldn't be allowed. All those scare stories from the States were a bit overwrought. Things were better regulated in Britain. Every gallon of water and every sack of chemicals had to be accounted for. Doing this had tortured Jamie every night of his offshore career - all twenty one nights of it. No, the Brits weren't as gung-ho as the Americans. They got on with the job quietly and effectively. Although when he thought about it, Jamie realised that they had quietly and effectively murdered the Toolpusher.

So they would drill on the green and there would be a bit of noise and a bit of light and a few trucks and a couple of demonstrators and a few chemicals and a bit of pumping. Then they would all go away and the wealthy residents of Foxhole Down could go back to counting their money and sipping their Upside Down.

Jamie knocked on the ancient door he'd been directed to, home of the friendly Fletcher family. It was opened by a severe and aggressive-looking man in a vest who was smoking.

'You want a smack in the teeth?' he asked, flicking the stub into Jamie's face.

Jamie blinked, realising that he's been the victim of yet another oilfield lie.

'Knock on the wrong door in these parts and you get a hiding. And you've knocked on the wrong door.' The man loomed large in the doorway.

86

Jamie, who considered himself to be from a hard town in the hard west coast of Scotland was having none of this. 'Who the hell are you, the village idiot? This isn't the Bronx. It's Foxhole Down.'

'It don't matter that they're all pussies round here. Doesn't make me any less hard.'

'I don't doubt it,' said Jamie. 'But I can't imagine that you've got many takers for a good old-fashioned punch-up in these parts.'

Fletcher's face fell. 'It's been shit since the McGeedys got evicted,' he said sadly. 'And that were twenty years ago.'

'You own this?'

Fletcher nodded.

'Must be worth a bit.'

'So what? We don't belong nowhere else.'

'Well it looks like your luck has changed,' said Jamie. 'That drillcrew is the biggest bunch of scumbags I've ever seen in my entire life.'

Fletcher's face came alive.

'We've just has a mass brawl. There's at least twenty guys you could pick a fight with. And most of them look like they'd nurse a pretty decent grievance too. You could have grudges flying about in all directions.'

Fletcher was so happy he looked like he was ready to give Jamie a big, gap-toothed kiss. 'Any chance of a job?'

'Ask the big American. No fighting on site, mind.'

'Fair enough.'

Jamie retreated, feeling pleased that he'd discovered the one household in the village that was glad to see them.

'What did you want?' said Fletcher.

'A room for the night. But it's okay. I know where I can sleep for free.'

*

The Vicar checked his swollen knuckles. He was curiously exhilarated after his fight with the Toolpusher. He felt that he had besmirched the cloth, but he also felt that the Lord would have been proud of him too. He had beaten that blasphemous, foul-mouthed hoodlum like a drum. There was a man who wouldn't be venturing into the woods any time soon, the Vicar thought, chuckling to himself. There was no getting away from the fact: a little violence made a man feel good.

Rooster entered the church.

'Reverend?'

The Vicar shot up from his kneeler. How brief his vainglorious moment had been. Of course he hadn't simply taken on one man, he'd taken on an entire crew. And now the vendetta was about to begin. The Vicar felt so stupid. How could he have imagined that there was any such thing as a little violence? Jesus lost his temper once, and they crucified him for it. Now, he was convinced, his own Calvary was about to begin.

'If it's about the Toolpusher,' the Vicar stammered, 'I'm so dreadfully sorry. He reacted rather badly to one of my mud bombs. Then he gave up the chase for the electrician and came over to me. Then he said some rude things about Jesus, which I took exception to. Then he asked me what I was going to do about it. And then I did something about it. And I was better at doing something about it than he was.'

'What did he say about Jesus?'

'He called him an effing chancer and started talking about him getting the leg over with Mary Magdalene.'

'Why that son-of-a...' Rooster checked himself before he swore in a holy place. 'Where I come from that's fighting talk.'

'So you understand?'

'I do.'

'And you forgive me?'

'Of course.'

The Vicar launched himself into Rooster's arms. 'Truly, you are a child of Christ,' he said.

'Well Amen to that,' said Rooster, who was a little taken aback. 'That must be the nicest compliment I've ever received. So you'll do the blessing?'

The Vicar contorted his face. 'Yes,' he said eventually.

Rooster took out his wad of cash. 'I guess there will be a fee?'

'No. I live simply. What remains of my life will be spent on a purely spiritual plane.' However, try as he might, the Vicar couldn't stop his face from lighting up at the sight of the money.

'Here,' Rooster thrust a bundle of cash into the Vicar's hands. 'I'm sure you can find others who'll have a use for it. I never heard of a church that wouldn't take cash.'

'Me neither,' said the Vicar ruefully.

Rooster watched as the Vicar counted the money, folded and pocketed it. Those hands have handled a few notes, he thought.

'I take it you're not planning to attack any other members of my crew?' said Rooster.

'No, I think I'll quit the fight game with an unbeaten record.'

'I've got some crew you really wouldn't want to get on the wrong side of. We'll do the blessing just before we break ground and start drilling. In a coupla days.' Rooster waved and left.

The Vicar sat down. He had some thinking to do. This was going to be a blessing that they would never forget.

*

Jamie breezed into the church with the breeze, accompanied by a crisp tumbling of dried leaves. The smell of lamb stew reminded Jamie that he'd forgotten to eat.

The Vicar loomed out of the darkness. 'Hungry?' he asked.

'Famished,' said Jamie, taking the place in. He wasn't sure whether the outside was coming inside, or if the inside had gone out. Nesting boxes had replaced statues in various nooks.

'Where have the saints gone?' said Jamie.

'That's a very profound question,' said the Vicar, his face alive to the possibilities of the answer. 'You could say that I've just been joined by one.'

Jamie smiled modestly. He loved flattery.

'I think this church could use a man like you,' said the Vicar.

Jamie looked around dubiously.

Seeing this, and feeling the need to justify himself, the Vicar added hopefully, 'I'm hoping to get a barn owl.'

'It's a fine barn,' said Jamie, 'as barns go.'

'It's a better church,' said the Vicar, 'as churches go.'

'It's not like any church I've ever seen.'

'Quite,' said the Vicar. 'Church of Scotland churches are quite …' the vicar searched for the right Scottish word, '… canny.'

'How did you know I was Church of Scotland?'

'You have a Presbyterian demeanour.'

Jamie smiled. He was being flattered again. 'Wait until you meet my girlfriend,' he said. 'She's Spanish.'

The vicar laughed - as if he'd just been told a joke, which he had. 'That's simply fabulous. You'll make a wonderful conundrum for each other. There's no point in having too many similarities.'

'Or any similarities whatsoever.'

'I like your Free Church of Scotland churches. They have no decorations at all. They're so bare, they're almost….'

'Minimalist,' said Jamie.

'Yes, but that makes them very religious. As are the most opulently decorated churches, like in Spain. It's the churches in the middle that don't work, the ones made to look like a suburban front room. Sadly, that's most of them.'

Jamie had thought that the Vicar was a lunatic. Now, he realised, he was simply an intelligent man who was a bit lonely.

'I'm seeking sanctuary,' said Jamie. 'It's an ancient and honourable church tradition. Until the cabin is plumbed-in and wired-up.'

The Vicar took a long look at Jamie. 'The door of this church is open to all living things. I'm going to need your help. I don't believe that you're a fracker at all.'

The Vicar led Jamie over to his cooking pot and handed him a ladle of succulent food. Jamie ate it greedily.

'Wow,' said Jamie. 'Perfection. Vicar, you have created an amazing stew.'

The Vicar smiled, his eyes glinting in the candlelight. 'I've plenty more stews where that came from.'

Chapter 14 – Such Stuff As Dreams Are Made On

Jennifer put the finishing touches to the barricade at her front door. It had come to this. The drill crew, quite clearly, were rapists and cut-throats. She wasn't going to be found in the morning on a blood-soaked bed with her legs akimbo, her face contorted into its final scream. That same blood boiled at the thought of her MP allowing such a thing in Foxhole Down. All those years banging on about law and order. Meaningless. Gone at the first whiff of profit. And to think that she'd thought that socialism was the enemy.

It had taken her almost two hours to move her furniture and ornaments to cover the windows and doors. Oh, how she needed a man. He could have managed it all in under half an hour. Then again, with a man there would have been no need for a barricade. As it was, she'd have happily spent the night with her arms wrapped around a shotgun. That said it all about men: they were either to be loved or shot. It wasn't a happy thought to carry to an empty bed with her.

It was like living in Stalingrad, waiting for the Germans. Or like living in Berlin, waiting for the Russians. But it was actually here in the loveliest part of England at the dawn of the 21st century. If Foxhole Down wasn't safe, nowhere was. The world had quite wilfully been allowed to run out of control. A deep and evil power was behind this.

Once she'd tucked herself up in bed, Jennifer permitted herself dreams of a better world, populated by better men, but run by women. Her debonair environmentalist was out there somewhere, a strong man most definitely in touch with his feminine side - and with his hands all over her feminine side too.

But looming in Jennifer's dreams was the spectre of Hamish, the wild and poetic Scot. A sworn enemy. A beast. The man who had lit the fuse of her sexuality. The rig crew had laughed cruelly at her, standing next to the statuesque Anouska. Hamish hadn't even broken a smile. He had looked up at her and tapped his heart with his fist. Then he had raised his fist in a "be strong" gesture. Or was it a horrible "red power" salute? It was odd, she had thought of oil workers as being extreme right wingers. There was nothing socialist about fracking. The man was a delightful cocktail of contradictions. He also looked vaguely familiar. And he'd written another letter.

My Dearest Angel, How my heart mocks me. Every beat that it makes, when it is not against your tender breast feels like a sledgehammer blow to a cement head by a deranged roustabout. I am in seven circles of hell and this fine little village becomes my own personal hellhole. It would take but one smile from you to transform it into a paradise. I tried to fight my way through the fight to fight for your honour but the drippy mud engineer got there first with a borrowed empty bottle. He is also from Scotland but not from the untamed passionate side. Had I got to your assailant I would not have required any weapons. My passion would have led me to tear him limb from limb bare-handed. I fear for your safety my love. This is the biggest bunch of murderous cut-throats I've ever come across. And that's saying something. I guess the oil industry really is scraping the bottom of the barrel. Fracking has a lot to answer for. I will warn them off, but a head of steam is building up, if you get my drift. Know that I will watch over you night and day, dreaming of forbidden kisses.

Jennifer didn't go to sleep with a shotgun. She went to sleep with Hamish's love letter tucked under her pillow, ready to explode.

*

Alan went to his own uneasy repose. His mind wouldn't leave him alone. He could sense the last end of his own life looming. Previous thoughts of another sedate decade in the mini paradise of Foxhole Down had been delusions, he now realised.

He was the man who had made things. Oh such things he had made! In many ways, he was like the village blacksmith. That was an honest trade. His own, less so.

Alan's life philosophy had been embodied in his cricket. How nobly he had played that most noble of games! He's played honestly and decently and with a smile on his face. He'd been as true as the pitches he'd rolled so relentlessly. He never questioned an umpire's decision. He never even waited on an umpire's decision when he knew he was out. He always walked. He applauded every good shot of opposing batsmen, every half century and century scored. There wasn't a bowler in Hampshire who hadn't received a nod of respect when they'd sent down a delivery that had bettered him. He'd never dreamed of cursing his opponents - "sledging" was the euphemism they'd given it. Its increasing use in the game had added some sombre notes to the last movement of his playing days.

The desecration of the green was nothing but sledging in physical form. It was a massive "Fuck You!" aimed at the very heart of the English soul. Yes. This wasn't an economic undertaking at all. It was a physical and psychological assault. It was the announcement of a new world order.

Alan stirred in his sheets.

There was only one question that needed to be answered: Who was behind this?

He was determined to find this out before they came for him, as he now knew they would. Things were always better found out from the inside. Alan would report to the site tomorrow and present himself for work.

There was a light tap tap tapping on his window. Rain, Alan imagined, was falling on Foxhole Down, falling on the future, falling on the past. Alan wondered whether he had actually been transported back in time to face his forefathers and explain himself. Perhaps the tap tap tapping was Blind Pew, come to tip him the Black Spot.

*

The Vicar bedded down in his cot with a deep sense of satisfaction. He had fought the good fight and provided sanctuary for a pilgrim.

There was definitely something of the Wandering Jew about Jamie. He was a man on the move. But to what or to where was his pilgrimage? It used to be so easy to choose. He would have taken the Pilgrim's Way to Canterbury. The Vicar wasn't even sure that Jamie himself knew where he was headed. Modern life had created too many options. He then, the Vicar, would send Jamie on his way. Onward Christian Soldiers.

The Vicar chuckled to himself. If ever there was an oxymoron, it was the idea of a Christian soldier. What an old fool he had been, getting into a fight. Sinning was so enjoyable. That was the problem – and therein lay humankind's entire struggle. The oil well on the village green was a sin in itself. He was sure that someone, somewhere, was having a very good time. Some devil was laughing at this mess. And just as the Almighty's plan was concealed from mankind, so too were the plans of those behind the drilling. The Vicar's eyes flicked open.

Someone was playing at God.

In this moment, the Vicar understood everything that was going on in Foxhole Down. What was going on had nothing to do with oil whatsoever.

The Vicar thought about his next sin. Where on earth was he going to place his first bomb?

*

Jamie could hear the birds flying above his head. He thought that there might be bats in the belfry. Then he realised that there was no belfry. There was certainly a large bird taking flight. It was probably an owl, but it wasn't twit-twooing on demand.

The Vicar had unrolled a makeshift mattress on the flagstones in front of the altar. He'd provided plenty of snug bedding and a wonderfully supportive feather pillow. Jamie couldn't have been more comfortable. He liked the austerity of his surroundings too. Antonia was in London on a nick-nack buying spree. She and her mother could undoubtedly have the church stuffed with tat in a matter of days. The churches in Spain, he thought, had been cluttered. They were definitely into their icons, which may as well have been idols for all that Jamie could tell. He reckoned that it had only taken a few name changes and a wardrobe update to recycle the old pagan gods into Christian saints. Give or take the odd Inquisition, things then rattled along much as they had done for the cavemen twenty thousand years before.

With thoughts of church furnishings swirling about his head and a silent owl swirling above his head, Jamie could feel himself drifting off to sleep. But he made an effort to stay awake. This was a bliss that he wanted to prolong. Foxhole Down was a delightfully Russian-free zone. They would never find him here. Once drilling was finished, he and Antonia could buy one of the small cottages. It would be a beautiful place to raise children – if the environment remained intact.

It was a big if.

Jamie knew that he would do what he could to minimise the damage that the crew would do. And what a crew. They hadn't been hired. They'd been auditioned. Who on earth had rounded that mob up? What were they thinking?

The combination of that drill crew and moving machinery was likely to be explosive. Jamie couldn't help but laugh. What an adventure this was. Getting involved in the oil business was the best thing he had ever done. It had been nothing but murder and mayhem from day one. How many people could say they were on the run for their lives? It sure beat the dreary nine-to-five economy hands down. Now it looked like he was working for a criminal too. Throw in a bunch of barking mad villagers, a sex-bomb international artist and a Vicar intent on saving his soul, and the possibilities for fun were endless.

As Jamie looked blissfully up at a darkened Jesus, he realised that there was only one question that required to be answered: Who was going to die?

*

Anouska lay with the gorgeous and quite naked Trudi snoozing in her arms. "Sapphic sex" eased you into the sensual world just by saying it. "Heterosexual sex" just didn't cut it aurally, or physically, in most cases. The sensual man was a rare thing. But there were still pleasures to be had there. She couldn't get the Vicar out of her head. And now other men were clambering in too. One of the drill crew – he seemed like management – had an aura. He was thin and young, wary and slightly nervous. There was something of the outlaw about him. He wore an easy sexuality like a new jacket. She had seen him go, late on, from the Fletchers' into the church.

Men. Men. Men. How they pleased her. What a world they had created with their inventions and their science and their war. They had given Anouska every convenience that she needed. She had indulged all of her desires and now she wanted for nothing. She was one of the luckiest women who had ever lived. And she knew it. She knew also that the age of men was coming to an end.

Mother Earth was calling a halt.

The mind-set was changing. The paradigm was shifting. The age of exploitation and rape was coming to a close. The sensual world was the only world and human beings would be eased into it as easily as your tongue eased its way around "Sapphic sex". Men didn't believe their own words any more. And their actions were increasingly lame.

This latest hole in the ground (Why were men so obsessed by holes?), no good would come of it. Anouska would make sure of that. Or rather, she would make sure that all kinds of good would come of it, just not the sort that the men were dreaming of. She smiled. It was time for different dreams.

And so, gathering her lover closer, Anouska allowed herself to slip beyond sensuality, towards dreams. And death.

Chapter 15 – Media Blitz

Anouska was all paint-spattered business the next morning. No make-up, hair like a rat's nest, wearing designer rags, she was still heart-breakingly glamorous – to Jennifer, who wanted to scream, "Please! Please! Please! Teach me! Teach me! Tell me your secrets. How is it done? I want to be like you! Help me! I'm begging you!"

If anyone wanted to make Jennifer get her tongue round "Sapphic sex", it was Anouska. She could feel herself blushing. Her own makeover was but a day away, but now she realised that she needed so much more than hair and make-up. She needed an expert on clothes. She needed an expert on accessories. No one accessorised like the continentals. She needed someone French or Italian. And boy, did she need an expert on men. But what she really needed, she reflected, was a psychologist. She had gotten everything wrong since her childhood and there was probably a lot wrong with her childhood too. No, what Jennifer really really needed was not to be Jennifer at all. She needed to be somebody else altogether. Oh dear.

Anouska, moving things on to a battle footing, and not trusting the intermittent mobile phone signals, had installed a bank of phones in the rectory. Before her sat Jennifer, Alan, Grassy Knoll and the Vicar.

'Listen up,' she said, sounding warlike. 'Today the gloves come off. This marks the beginning of an all-out media assault on our enemies. I've got the national contacts, so I'm going to get them down here and we'll make a big splash. There will be radio cars. There will be television crews. I'll be the main focus. Accept that. Put your egos to one side. And live with it. They ain't coming down here for the glory of nature. With these boys it's always human interest and I'm the most interesting human here. Sorry. It's brutal. But there you are.'

'Where does that leave the rest of us?' said Grassy Knoll irritably.

Anouska tossed her magnificent mane. 'What you are is "local colour".'

The "local colour" sat gormlessly in front of her.

'They might want to interview you for short inserts into the main story. Your job is to look middle class and pathetic.'

'I think we can manage that,' said Grassy Knoll dryly.

'We're going to pitch this as a dagger to the beating heart of Olde England. A national catastrophe. The rape of our way of life. Evil foreign oil companies succeeding where Hitler and Napoleon failed. Did Winston Churchill die for this?'

'Winston Churchill died of old age,' said Alan.

'You know what I mean,' Anouska snapped. She was waving her hands about, pacing in front of them, in full flow. 'We want to make it clear to the world that if Foxhole Down isn't worth fighting for, then Britain's fucked.'

'Britain is fucked,' said Grassy Knoll.

'I don't want defeatist talk round here,' said Anouska. 'And that reminds me, I'm going to get international press on board too. We need to find out who the money behind this really is, see if we can flush the bastards out into the open and take them on.'

'If it would help, I could dress up as a Morris Dancer,' said Alan.

'I'm liking it,' said Anouska. 'That's exactly the kind of thinking we need. Pagan and ancient. Vicar, we need you for the Christian angle.'

'There's a Christian angle?' said the startled Vicar, pulling a twig from his hair. 'Oh yes. Do unto others.'

'No, not that rubbish,' said Anouska. 'Christianity itself under threat from dark forces. Hints at a Muslim takeover. That ought to rouse them in the shires.'

'So we're fighting dirty?' said the Vicar.

'Is there any other way to fight?' said Anouska.

'There are many paths to God,' the Vicar beamed.

'I'll bet there are,' said Anouska, toying with a loose strand of hair. 'And I can think of one in particular. Anyway,' she said, gathering herself and handing each person two sheets of paper, 'here's a list of numbers for each of you to call. They are all local press and social groups: newspapers; radio stations; bloggers; churches; chambers of commerce; sports clubs. On the second sheet, is a script prepared by my public relations experts in London. Use this. The language is specially selected for maximum impact and maximum effectiveness. Try and make it sound natural. Does anyone have any questions?'

It was Jennifer who spoke.

'Do you think I should bonk Hamish the Scotsman?'

Anouska covered the Vicar's ears. She leaned over and whispered in Jennifer's ear. 'Don't bonk him, darling. Fuck him senseless.'

*

'Fracking?' said a weary voice. 'What's the angle?'

'The angle,' said Grassy Knoll, 'is that evil foreigners of unknown identity are tearing up the heart of England, poisoning our drinking water and there is nothing we can do to stop them.'

'We need something more. Our readers are a bit fracked-out.'

'We've got Anouska de Gaulle.'

'Naked?'

'Why would she be naked?'

'Because that's what it's going to take to get the story into our newspaper.'

'There's a drilling rig on Foxhole Down's village green! Are you telling me that that's not news?'

''We don't sell a lot of copies in Foxhole Down.'

'You don't sell any copies in Foxhole Down. The shop closed seven years ago. That doesn't mean that we don't buy any.'

'To be honest, it would be difficult to generate much sympathy for Foxhole Down. It's full of rich incomers, rich inbred locals – and the Fletcher family. If fracking's going to happen anywhere, Foxhole Down's as good a place as any. It's out of everybody's way. Nice to see the wealthy suffering for a change. If you can guarantee me a shot of the de Gaulle bitch in floods of tears as they spill toxic sludge over her rhododendrons, we might be talking.'

'Who owns your newspaper?' asked Grassy, changing tack.

'It's a corporation. We got taken over.'

'Enough said.' Grassy hung up.

'I've had exactly the same responses,' sighed Alan. 'The churches aren't even interested. The attitude seems to be that so long as it's not in their back yard…'

'It's every village for themselves,' said the Vicar. 'They came for the Jews, but I did nothing because I wasn't a Jew. They came for the communists but I did nothing because I wasn't a communist. They came for the queers but I did nothing because I wasn't a queer. When they came for me I cried "Help!" but there was no one left to come.'

'Oh Vicar,' Grassy Knoll wailed, 'if only we'd supported the miners, none of this need ever have happened.'

'There's no need to be cynical,' said the Vicar.

'Cynicism is all we have left.'

*

And so they ploughed on, creating their own peculiar furrow of futility. At the merest whiff of controversy, the local media ran for the unfracked hills.

'Isn't there a journalist left who want to get his teeth into a juicy controversy?' the Vicar asked.

'They've been weeded out over the last twenty years,' replied Grassy Knoll. 'And staff cuts mean that even the remaining timid ones don't have time to get their teeth into anything.'

'That's one of your more plausible conspiracy theories,' said Alan.

'The biggest controversy Foxhole Down ever had was some suspicious judging at the gymkhana,' said Grassy Knoll.

'Just when we need a free press, we discover we haven't got one,' said Alan.

'We never thought we'd have a fire, but an arsonist came to the village,' said the Vicar. 'And when we opened up the fire station, the hoses were perished and the crew petrified.'

There were some glimmers of hope. The Vicar, peeved at Grassy Knoll's cynicism, actually got in touch with some miners in Yorkshire, or rather, some ex-miners in Yorkshire. They, alas, were more preoccupied with providing for local food banks in their own area. They did, however, pledge solidarity to Foxhole Down's "cause" and sent a rousing rendition of "The Red Flag" down the line. Even Grassy Knoll was touched.

But it was Jennifer who delivered the most radical support: the North Hampshire Knitting Circle vowed to put their needles together for justice in Foxhole Down.

'Never mind,' said Alan. 'Anouska's going to get us the big splash we require nationally.'

*

The female Reporter walks along in front of the cottages and the pub, making Foxhole Down look like the unspoilt rural paradise that it had so recently been.

'Imagine that you are a hugely rich, hugely successful artist. You'd want to live somewhere like here, wouldn't you?' he begins.

They show a shot of Anouska's priory and then cut back to the Reporter.

'And if you'd made your fortune from Confronting Disappointment, what you wouldn't want to confront would be this.'

The Reporter points to her right and the camera dutifully pans to show the rig on the green.

Cut to Anouska in her front room, smoking and looking fabulous. 'I mean, they threw a fence round the green and then the next thing they dug it up, put a load of stones over it and then a drilling rig showed up.'

Cut to a "noddy shot" of the Reporter nodding sympathetically in Anouska's front room.

Back on Anouska: 'There was nothing we could do to stop it.'

Back on the Reporter: 'Were you disappointed?'

Back on Anouska: 'This isn't just about the village, it's about everybody in the country.'

Back on the Reporter, almost winking at the camera: 'Yes, but were you disappointed?'

Back on Anouska: 'We're living under a tyranny.'

The Reporter, now openly mugging at the camera, 'For the last time Anouska, were you DISAPPOINTED?'

Anouska's face crumples, looking almost comic. Then there's a jump cut. 'Totally gutted.'

Cut back to the Reporter with the rig behind her. 'She may have paid for her expensive pile by confronting disappointment, but you try getting the artist to actually say the word herself.'

Cut to Fletcher. 'I don't have a problem with it. It's bringing jobs and a bit of excitement to the place. I cashed my cheque this morning.' He gives a big, not enough teeth, grin.

Cut to a well-heeled incomer. 'They've been perfectly straightforward about what's going on. I don't see the problem. I know there's a few people up in arms about it, but they're the disaffected types that hang around the pub.'

Cut to the Vicar outside the pub. 'There are many paths to salvation,' he says, cheerily.

Back on the Reporter on the green, as a diesel generator revs behind her, sending up a plume of smoke. 'At least the local vicar is staying on-message. Just a tip to any prospective artists out there. If you want to avoid confronting disappointment on your own doorstep, don't buy your pile in a village that just sold its own green to an oil company.'

*

'The bastards,' said Anouska. 'We've been stitched up. She never once mentioned disappointment to me. She recorded those questions when I was out of the room.'

'They've edited me to look like a complete buffoon,' said the Vicar.

'They left out everything I said about the sinister conspiracy,' said Grassy Knoll.

Anouska paced about in a rage. They had assembled in the pub and had watched the report on the newly-installed sixty-five inch TV screen. 'I've been made to look like a complete fool,' Anouska fumed. 'So much for public service broadcasting. They even put us in the comedy slot at the end, the bit reserved for skateboarding cats!'

Anouska ran to the front door and launched her pint of champagne at the rig. Then she started yelling at the derrick.

'Congratulations boys! Another hard-on! Always worried about getting it up, aren't you? Always worried about size! The biggest cock that Foxhole Down's ever seen. Higher than the church. Says it all. Your erection towers over the best that Jesus could achieve! How big does that make you, boys?'

Rooster, a couple of his thieving/pimp/fire-starting colleagues, and Jamie gathered to watch.

'Gonna make a hole, boys? It was bad enough when you just wanted to fuck women. Now you're fucking everything! Fucking the green. Fucking the air we breathe. Fucking the water we drink. Fucking our view. Fucking our newspapers. Fucking our television. Fucking our minds with your mealy-mouthed fucking opinions. I'm amazed you haven't fucked the ducks in the fucking duck pond! Is there anything you wouldn't fuck?'

Some of the drill crew shook their heads. It didn't help Anouska's mood.

'Go fuck yourself, you planet-fucking perverts! Every misery brought to this world comes courtesy of you and your ridiculous genitals. If I was a man I'd kill myself, just so there'd be one less of you! Listen to me! You might have the media in your pocket. You might have the politicians in your pocket. You might have the money in your pocket. But you don't have me in your oily fucking pockets! I am an artist! I create my own world, Goddammit! I will visit seven circles of hell on you. You don't get to fuck me. I'm gonna fuck you! Fuck you! Fuck you!'

The Vicar jerked Anouska backwards. She made to swing for him, but saw the collar and stopped. Instead she contented herself with kicking over a new sign, which promised: "Champions League Live". The Vicar hustled her back into the pub.

'God, I'd love a night in bed with her,' said Rooster.

'I couldn't agree more. But by the time she'd finished with you, you'd need about fifty stitches,' said Jamie.

'Even better.'

Back in the pub, Alan had some more devastating news.

'You know the protesters that we were going to mobilise?'

Anouska nodded dumbly.

'Well they can't come. There seems to be a number of problems. The benefits cuts and the sanctions regime have cut the number of people available to protest. Some of the most vulnerable have been driven to their deaths. We're not the easiest place to get to, so cost is an issue. The other problem is that there are so many environmental issues kicking off around the country that there aren't enough protesters to go round.'

Anouska blinked. 'You're telling me there's a national shortage of crusties?'

Alan nodded.

'So we're alone?'

Alan nodded.

'Then we are well and truly fucked,' said the Vicar.

At this, the bomb went off.

Chapter 16 - The Bombshell

The police were going to divide the suspects into two groups. Those with a criminal record (the entire drill crew and the Fletchers) were to be interviewed first. The others were to be interviewed later. However, checking out the drill crew's records proved problematical. Some of the files were so big that the FBI had problems e-mailing them. A request for a "highlights" page of the most serious crimes was turned down.

'If you need to ask, you really don't want to know,' said the Bureau's UK Liaison officer.

'How bad can it be?' said the Desk Sergeant at the local police station.

'As bad as it gets,' came the reply. 'Have you heard of the scum of the earth?'

'Yes.'

'Well these boys make the scum of the earth look like The Waltons.'

'Where do you suggest we start?'

'They're all accomplished liars. They'll give you the runaround. You could waste months. Be careful who you arrest.'

They were careful who they arrested. They arrested Jamie.

*

'Why are all policemen world-weary?' said Jamie.

'It's the rancid tea we drink,' said Inspector Witcher, stirring his tea world-wearily. 'The millionth Styrofoam cup and the billionth plastic spoon – which has a functional life of fifteen seconds,' he added jadedly.

Inspector Witcher tossed the spoon into Rooster's bin and squared up to Jamie. 'You arrive on an oil rig. The Toolpusher is bludgeoned to death and tossed into a mud pit – a pit that you are responsible for. The derrickman is subsequently found murdered in Cornwall. You and the Spanish logger, meanwhile, have disappeared off the face of the earth. Less than a year later, you arrive here and a bomb goes off.'

'And here was me hoping for the quiet life,' said Jamie.

'Seems like one coincidence too many for my liking,' said Witcher, taking a seat and easing back in it. 'Let's hear it. I'm all ears.'

'I would have been happy if it had all stopped at the Toolpusher's murder,' said Jamie. 'He was a nasty piece of work.'

'Heaven forfend,' said Witcher cynically.

'He was actually murdered by the derrickman. Meanwhile, I accidentally added several tonnes of Russian-owned cocaine to the mud system, thinking it was chalk. Cue angry Russian gangsters. Hence disappearing off the face of the earth with beautiful Spanish logger. Mucho jiggy-jiggy in a hacienda in Catalonia – without satellite telly. Russian gangsters catch up with derrickman in Cornwall. Almost catch up with us. Flee for our lives. Tour of Spain. Lots more jiggy-jiggy. Gorgeous Spanish logger reckons best place to hide is on a land job in England. Nobody will ever find us in deepest Hampshire. Then a bomb goes off.'

'My world-weary detective skills tell me that every word of that is true,' said Witcher.

'Blimey,' said Jamie.

'It was the "jiggy-jiggy" that sealed it. It's the kind of pathetic boastfulness that liars never think to add.'

'When you think you're facing imminent horrible death, you can't keep your hands of each other,' said Jamie.

'Who do you think planted the bomb?'

'It wasn't the Vicar. I slept with him in the church last night.'

Witcher raised an eyebrow. 'More jiggy-jiggy?'

'Certainly not!' said Jamie. 'I'd never do it in a church. That would be sacrilege. I'd be cursed. Antonia would leave me. And I wouldn't do it with a vicar either. Not a male one. A female one would have to be pretty hot to tempt me. It's something about the collar. It's a real turn off.'

'I guess the outfit isn't designed to get people into a state of sexual frenzy,' said Witcher. 'You're beginning to ramble and make a fool of yourself. Another classic sign of innocence.'

'I need a favour from you,' said Jamie. 'I need you to keep quiet about my background and about our presence here. We can't afford news leaking to Russia.'

'I need a favour from you,' said Witcher. 'I need a pair of eyes and ears on the site. Let me know of anything unusual that goes on amongst the crew. I may ask you to watch specific individuals. And I want your logging lumberjack girlfriend to keep an eye on the villagers for me.'

'Sounds reasonable,' said Jamie.

But it didn't sound reasonable at all.

*

Rooster surveyed the damage. The bomb had been placed in a steel container used to hold spare generator parts. Luckily, it had succeeded only in blowing the top off. Experts confirmed that there was nothing unusual in the type of explosive used.

'I bet Vladimir Putin and the Ayatollah are glad to be in the clear,' Rooster said. 'But I wouldn't put it past our politicians to blame 'em anyway.'

He turned to see Alan standing beside him.

'I'm looking for a job,' said Alan.

'No shit,' said Rooster.

'I used to run my own company. I'm a logistics expert. The bomb's already gone off. Inspector Witcher has just given me a clean bill of health. I figure that if it's impossible to stop you drilling this well, by working here I can at least minimise the damage you do.'

They were distracted by the arrival of a large truck bearing two enormous tanks. The tanks were emblazoned with a gigantic skull and crossbones, under which, in equally enormous letters, was the word "Toxic".

'You're hired, old man,' said Rooster. 'A logistics man is exactly what I need. Because it looks like the fracking fluid has arrived. And we don't need that shit for another four weeks.'

Alan looked at the tanks in utter horror. He hadn't arrived a moment too soon. 'I'll send it back,' he said.

*

The Vicar was staring at the toxic tanks when he was arrested.

Witcher took him in for questioning. In fact, Witcher took him into his own church for questioning.

The Vicar was pleased at Witcher's reaction to this temple of decay. As Witcher took in the church, so the Vicar took in Witcher. He was a man in the early years of middle age. He was smart in appearance without being fastidious. His clothes were neat and showed no signs of wear and tear. They could easily have been more stylish. The Inspector's eyes were bright, undimmed by years of low wattage work. This was a man who could create his own stimulation. He was, the Vicar thought, a man of potential. Strangely, he also seemed a little world-weary.

'Do you understand why you've been arrested, Vicar?' Witcher asked.

'I punched the Toolpusher.'

'You went on the internet and searched for home-made bombs.'

'I don't have the internet.'

Witcher looked at the Vicar world-wearily. 'Don't make me explain how I know that it was you in the pub, with the computer, at half past four, three days ago. Searches for bomb information tend to set off alarms in strange places.'

'I can imagine,' said the Vicar. 'Although obviously I couldn't three days ago. I've been rather naïve.'

'You didn't plant the bomb, did you?'

'Not on this occasion.'

'Any other interactions with the drillcrew?'

'Threw a few mud, er, bombs.'

'I'd stay away if I were you. They're a scurvy bunch. Direct from central casting. God knows who hired them. They certainly weren't thinking about local sensibilities. Thieves to a man. I'd start to lock the church if I were you.'

'Anything that the church has of value, they are welcome to.'

'They'd steal Jesus himself if they thought they could get a price.'

Witcher looked around some more. Whatever fixtures and fittings were left held no value. It was only the stained glass windows that were worth anything. Locking the door wouldn't make any difference to them.

'You've got yourself a back-to-basics place here, Vicar.'

'The locals have been very kind. The goodly people of Foxhole Down are givers rather than takers.'

'And the badly men of the drillcrew are the Brotherhood of Perpetual Pilfering. It's not looking good for this village. There are more lions than Christians, that's for sure.'

The Vicar spoke with commendable grace and humility. 'What will be will be. My time on this earth is short,' he said.

'Oh don't go all Jesus on me,' said Witcher, who wasn't in a commending mood. 'We're not looking for another crucifixion. If we're not careful, there's going to be a murder or a rape. Explosions will be the least of our worries.'

'Are you going to take me to the station?'

'No Vicar. You're un-under arrest. I reckon the bomb was an inside job. The roof of that container had been deliberately weakened. Made sure the explosion went upwards and no one got hurt. There's something far more sinister than you at work. We won't be needing your bombs after all.'

'I'll bear that in mind.'

'Where bombs are concerned, stick to the mud, Vicar. The bomb investigation is closed. But you'll see me around the village. I'd imagine that all kinds of interesting things are about to happen.'

*

Alan and Rooster struck up a rapport straight away.

Alan got himself ensconced in one half of Rooster's office, which was in itself one half of Rooster's trailer. The other half was Rooster's accommodation area, which comprised a bedroom, kitchen and toilet like Jamie's, only twice the size and without the filth. The office had two desks, two phones, two computers and, crucially, an enormous whiteboard. Alan loved whiteboards. They let you look at the bigger picture.

Alan and Rooster were soul mates. They were men of action, men of machinery, men who understood the motivations of men. They were men who made things. They were the drivers, in Europe and America, of the latter half of the 20th century. Similar men in China and India and Asia were the drivers of the opening half of the 21st. They were men of great ability, methodical men, men of limited imagination. They were men like Albert Speer, the armaments minister in Germany from 1942 to 1945. They were technocrats.

Rooster was a man who made oil wells. Alan was a man who made other things.

'The key thing to drilling a land well,' said Rooster, 'is site management. We've got to get equipment here in timely fashion and then get its ass out of here as soon as we're finished with it. Create the space before the next load of shit arrives. It's all about timing.'

Alan could feel his talents re-activating. Why did he ever think that he could end his days happily by counting his money, sipping the occasional pint and watching his beloved green go to seed? He was the one who had truly been going to seed. When they'd dug up the green, they'd excavated his brain too. If he was going to die, then he was going to die in harness. He couldn't go back to what he'd done before. He'd have to find something useful as a goal. First, there was a well to be drilled and a green to be restored.

The whiteboard was filling up quite nicely: key telephone numbers of suppliers; a list of key events; a list of equipment and personnel crucial to those events.

'I like your style, Colonel,' said Rooster, surveying the board. 'I could have done with you thirty years ago. Finally, I can see the big picture.'

There was a knock at the door. A Latino man came in. He was limping. Alan felt his blood chilling.

'This is Carlos, the derrickman,' Rooster said.

Alan and Carlos nodded to one another. Alan didn't want to make the man walk across the room. Clearly, he had an artificial leg.

Carlos caught sight of the whiteboard and spent a moment taking it in.

'Muy bien. Muy bien,' he said. 'But you have missed one thing. We need more racks for the additional drill pipe. After the 17 ½ inch section.'

Alan dutifully added this to the board. He wasn't even sure what a 17 ½ inch section was.

'Boss, the boys are getting restless. The whore situation is critical.'

Alan then did something that he never would have imagined ever doing. He went over to the whiteboard and at the top of the list wrote "Whores".

'If it's on the board, it's gonna happen,' said Rooster. 'Anything else.'

Carlos shook his head.

'Get out.'

Carlos limped off.

'You gotta be ruthless,' said Rooster. 'Especially with a cut-throat crew like this. Or guess whose throat is gonna get cut?'

Alan could imagine only too well. When he came in, Carlos had given him exactly the same look that Anouska had given him at the fancy dress party as Long John Silver. Carlos knew.

Chapter 17 - Finding Fault

Grassy Knoll sat himself down in front of his computer to pursue his favourite pastime. He was going to check out another conspiracy theory. Over years and ever since he'd been a teenager, he'd checked out just about every crackpot theory going. He'd checked out the dead Kennedys, the inside job on 911, the asset grab of the Iraq war, the Illuminati (naturally), the alien lizard theory of global domination, the military industrial complex, the prison industrial complex, left wing bias in the media, right wing bias in the media, the death of Diana, the death of Elvis, the death of Shergar, the faked moon landing, the Roswell flying saucer, the secret services' brain washing program MK-Ultra, who Shakespeare really was, who Paul McCartney really was, who Shergar really was, he looked into chemtrails, the death of snails, horoscopes and entrails. He hadn't bothered his arse with global warming or, for that matter, fracking. They were too scientific. Now the conspiracy chickens had come home to roost. It was time to check fracking out.

Grassy didn't have to look very hard. This, in part, was the reason he hadn't investigated it before. There was no challenge.

Fracking was a process whereby a toxic cocktail of sand, water and chemicals were forced at high pressure into tight rock formations to force them open and so allow trapped hydrocarbons to flow.

So far, so good.

The problem arose with what went in to the fracking fluid. It wasn't nice stuff. There was mercury, uranium, lead, benzene, toluene, ethylene glycol, radium, methanol, hydrochloric acid, formaldehyde and other things which went by the name of Unknown Volatile Organic compounds, or UVOs.

Grassy knew all about UFOs. They weren't here and he didn't believe in them. UVOs were here and were very real. It didn't matter whether Grassy Knoll believed in them or not.

The good news was that the toxic cocktail was pumped at least 10,000 feet underground. The bad news was that it didn't always go where it was supposed to.

Sometimes it came back up.

It was the old perennial: the law of unintended consequences. Fracking fluid was finding itself into water supplies. Two hundred and forty three private drinking wells had been contaminated in Pennsylvania alone. Benzene had got into an aquifer in Wyoming. The scary thing was that these were facts that Grassy had discovered in a single search.

It got worse still.

There were 40,000 gallons of fracking fluid used per well. And between one and 8 million gallons of water. The town of Barnhart in Texas had run out of water completely. They blamed fracking. So did Grassy Knoll.

Then there were the earthquakes: the contentious one in Lancashire, following the deformed well which had illegally not been reported to the government; or the 800 earthquakes in Arkansas that looked highly suspicious.

It got even worse again.

In Dish, Texas people were complaining of nausea, headaches, breathing difficulties, chronic eye and throat irritation. And brain disorders. If there were brain disorders in Foxhole Down, it was debateable whether anyone would notice. Grassy chuckled at that. Then he read on and stopped laughing. Fifteen different fracking chemicals had been detected in Dish's air. Trees were dying, horses were ill.

All of this was happening in America, where the shale deposits were huge and relatively faultless. In England, the rock formations were very faulty. And more likely to contaminate ground water with fracking fluid.

And it wasn't just the fracking fluid. There were numerous reports of leaking methane causing all kinds of health problems in areas of drilling.

Methane, Grassy knew, was one of the worst greenhouse gases.

This led logically to climate change. The mass of scientific evidence was overwhelming: the climate was changing. The system was so complex that nobody had a bloody clue how it was all going to pan out. What was definite was that human beings were in the midst of conducting a massive experiment on the climate upon which civilisations were depending. Carbon dioxide, historically at 275 parts per million, was now over 400. The oceans were 40% more acidic. These facts were undeniable.

Someone had calculated that for climate safety only 20% of the hydrocarbons already discovered could be consumed. It was the words "already discovered" that sealed the deal for Grassy. He wasn't a scientist, but he couldn't fault the logic nor the calculation.

The major oil companies were not climate change deniers. But Grassy Knoll spotted one major denial that the oil companies certainly were in: their share price. If they were truly serious about climate change, he reckoned, then their share price would have been written down. They were telling the market that they intended to burn every single barrel.

In that scenario, humankind was finished.

But what this told Grassy Knoll more than anything was that there was no need for further exploration. There was no need to be fracking at all. And the oil industry knew it.

Grassy sat back and lit a joint.

In all his years playing the stock market, Grassy had never thought beyond the balance sheet. The consequences of the actions of the companies that he had invested in had never troubled him. There were profits, but there were no ramifications. Capitalism kept its dirty secrets well-hidden and now he understood why.

Clearly, this was a conspiracy right on his own doorstep and clearly Grassy Knoll hadn't a clue what to do.

Grassy took a deep and blissful lungful of smoke. The marijuana worked its magic. Grassy felt the shackles fall from his mind. He knew exactly what he was going to do. He was going to do nothing.

Chapter 18 - Last Orders

The Major stood, polishing a glass as cannily as he had once polished his vowels. Events had taken a spectacular turn. To his left was a lounge, crowded with drilling types. To his right was a snug, crowded with locals. Through the back was a kitchen, lucratively pumping out meals and snacks 24/7. Above him were rooms, hastily refurbished and ready to let out at exorbitant rates to managerial drilling types. They were sure to come.

Instead of sneaking away from the village with a whimper, the Major was certain to leave with a bang. A couple of months of fracking money was just the boost his pension fund needed. He wasn't worried in the least about the pub losing property value because of the activity. Adjustments could be made. Bushes could be planted. Incomers didn't care.

Property prices in Spain had collapsed and Spain was where he was going; somewhere near the Costa del Crime. Dodgy characters were much more interesting. Nothing in life was as tedious as a self-made businessman. He'd heard them boasting in bars from Girona to Gibraltar. Crooks don't boast and the Major wanted a quiet life. He'd find himself a merry young widow and have himself a merry old retirement.

Prospects for a phony British Army Major-cum-landlord could not have been brighter.

Then Antonia walked in.

'Would you happen to know where I could get some accommodation?'

The Major beamed.

In the snug, Anouska, alerted by the Spanish accent, looked through. The door framed Antonia perfectly, showing off her lithe figure and aquiline neck. Anouska noted the classic Mediterranean features, the nose a little long, eyes a little wide. Antonia had been shopping in London and had found some designers that the High Street hadn't. Anouska knew that the oilfield paid well, but she also knew that it didn't pay that well.

The artist was intrigued, and not a little turned on.

Jamie arrived and the couple exchanged a kiss. Jamie ran a hand casually down Antonia's neck and back. Clearly, they would be making love soon.

Looking into Antonia's dreamy eyes, the world made sense to Jamie. Nothing needed to be said. She was so beautiful when she wasn't talking.

Anouska loomed in the doorway. 'Would you two like to come,' she let the word hang in the air, 'and join the locals?'

Antonia and Anouska exchanged a lingering look.

'You don't have to stay on your side,' Anouska teased. 'You can come over to my side any time you like.'

Antonia broke off eye contact. She could feel herself starting to blush. The Logger was intrigued, and not a little turned on.

Even Jamie the Mud Engineer was intrigued, and massively turned on.

'Sure,' Antonia's eyes shone. She cocked her shoulder sexily at Jamie. 'Let's go.' Antonia took Jamie's hand.

They went into the snug. As far as Jamie was concerned, they may as well have been entering a parallel universe.

They took a seat beside Anouska in the crooked corner. Two pints of beer materialised in front of them.

'This is Upside Down,' said Jamie.

'I'm an artist. I live in the old rectory that overlooks the village. Feel free to come and visit me whenever you want. Mi casa es su casa.'

Anouska was all over them like an erotically scented balm.

'I'd love to paint you,' she continued. 'You are a classic beauty.'

This was probably the most flattering thing that anyone had ever said to Antonia.

It was definitely the most flattering thing that anyone had ever said to Jamie. He thought that Anouska was talking to him.

'Do you want me naked?' he said.

Antonia and Anouska laughed.

'Whores! Whores!' Alan had arrived. He was agitated. And shouting. 'I need to find some whores!'

'Don't look at me,' said Jamie.

'Don't look at me,' said Anouska.

'You're an artist,' Alan stammered. 'You know these things.'

'If I were Pablo Picasso, you might be right. Sadly, I'm not.' Anouska turned to Antonia. 'Do you know that you look like one of Picasso's Desmoiselles d'Avignon?'

'Yes, one of the two figures in the middle. I see it. They were whores in Barcelona. You are saying that I look like a Barcelona whore?'

Anouska then made a sound that no one in the village had ever heard before: she giggled girlishly.

Jamie couldn't help himself. His mind was filling with ideas about threesomes.

'Somebody help me! I need to find whores for the drillcrew. There's a sexual time-bomb about to go off!'

'Sounds like more fun than the last bomb,' said Anouska.

'It won't be when you're dragged shrieking into the bushes.' Alan wobbled and slumped into a chair. 'I can't believe than I'm saying these words. I'm actually looking for whores.'

'Welcome to the oil patch,' said Jamie.

Anouska glared at Alan. 'You've joined the other side?'

'So have you, by the look of it. My excuse is that I can minimise the damage from the inside. What's yours?'

'I'm a sucker for beauty,' said Anouska. 'Someone get this man a drink.'

Jamie passed his virgin pint to Alan, who gulped gratefully.

'Do you know anything about the one-legged man?' Alan asked.

'A word to the wise,' said Jamie. 'With drilling types, it's best to keep talk light. Sports. Cars. Cake recipes. Believe me, you do not want to start getting into these guys' personal lives. They don't specialize in "Happy Ever After" stories. If you ask Carlos about how he lost his leg, he'll tell you some horrific tale about a blind transvestite prostitute, a crippled midget, a gangrenous pimp and an acid-throwing nun. The worst of it is, it'll probably be true.'

Antonia patted Alan's leg. 'Best not ask,' she whispered.

On Alan's other side, Grassy Knoll woke up. He was drunk. 'They're all out to get us!' he shouted.

There was a gasp. It came from the lounge. Jennifer had sashayed in. She'd had her makeover.

*

Alan sat at home, alone, staring out at the green, or rather, staring out at the oil rig which had been erected on the green. His new place of work. As garish as one of the tarts that he was supposed to find. He was a man used to sourcing chemicals and containers and small-scale electronics. Now it was drillpipe and rigwash and prostitutes.

If he didn't find any ladies of the night, he could only imagine what would happen to the ladies of the village. He could either inflict a plague of whores on Foxhole Down, or watch as its women were gang raped.

But it was Carlos, his one-legged nemesis, who worried Alan most. He would likely break the door down and come after him with a meat cleaver. It would be an horrific death, a gory end to a gory life.

Alan knew that his life was already over. There was no cricket, no green and no peace of mind for his retirement now.

It was time to head for the oven.

*

Grassy Knoll sat in his chair staring out at the toxic tanks. He knew that his life was over. He was headed for forty. He had no family. He knew no love. His perfect corner of the world was being destroyed in front of his very eyes. He had neither the wit nor the imagination to live happily.

He'd been happy to profit from the destruction of other parts of the world. Now he was watching other, equally anonymous, equally callous investors profiting from the destruction of his world. Capitalism had finally caught up with him. Grassy Knoll was the victim of his own conspiracy theory. It was a bitter truth.

He had lived by the sword. It was time to die by the sword.

Grassy Knoll wondered how long it would take for his body to be discovered. He'd probably be black by then. That would be embarrassing. Logically, Grassy realised that it was difficult to be embarrassed when you were dead, but he still didn't fancy it.

Then there were the issues of his suicide note and his will.

Suicide notes, he felt, were embarrassing in themselves. Full of self-pity and self-justification. If he were to write anything, it would have to be jaunty, which was kind of self-defeating for a suicide note.

Having never confronted his own mortality, he hadn't bothered to write a will. He was intestate, or he would be in about fifteen minutes. When he was dead.

He figured that something hastily written would be acceptable to a court. He could nip over to the rig and get a couple of the drilling boys to witness it. Those cut-throats wouldn't bat an eyelid, particularly if he bunged them a couple of hundred quid each. It would be his last financial transaction. This cheered him a little. There was something Shakespearean about it.

But who to leave his assets to? Alan and Jennifer were too rich for it to matter. The Major was a shameless profiteer. The Vicar would squander it on the poor. Grassy couldn't countenance giving it to any charities. More embarrassment. Acknowledgement of the fact that he'd had so little human interaction. What an utter waste of a life his life had been.

Then it hit him: Anouska. She would do something creative with it. She'd throw a fabulous party, with an enormous firework display and an amazing array of exotic drinks, exotic men and exotic women. This was exactly what he should have been doing with it. There would be enough for forty fabulous parties.

With a little piece of mind behind him, Grassy turned to the method. Pools of blood were out. Poison required some planning and he didn't particularly want to hang around. And he didn't want to hang around dying either, so hanging was out. He had no gun and he didn't fancy spreading his brains around his home if he did. He didn't want to drown in his own bath. He quite fancied carbon monoxide poisoning, but there was no guarantee that he wouldn't wake up in the morning. Besides, the boiler had just been serviced.

He'd spent his entire life asking the wrong type of questions. Now he only had one question left. And he couldn't answer it. He had to smile. Then he realised that the answer was right in front of him: the rig. The derrick.

He would climb it and jump off. Not only would he be guaranteed a swift end and a quick discovery, he'd shut the site down for a couple of days to boot. It might even generate a few headlines. It was a win-win situation.

Grassy Knoll felt at peace. No more questions. He had sobered up and was ready to die.

It was then that Grassy Knoll asked the question that would save his life.

*

When Grassy burst into Alan's house, Alan's head was in the oven.

'Alan! No! Oh God, I'm too late! No!'

Alan reversed out of the oven and raised his head. 'Don't you know it's rude not to knock? Let alone burst uninvited into my house? Honestly!'

Grassy swept Alan up into his arms. 'I've not got here a moment too soon. Don't do it Alan! Please!'

'Will you let me go?'

'Never, Alan! I'll never let you go. You're my friend forever!'

'Well, that's very kind of you Grassy, but…'

'No Alan, it's not kindness. I can't let you do this to yourself. I saw the state you were in at the pub. I had to come. You were the question that saved my life. I'm not here a moment too soon. Thank God!'

Grassy slowly released Alan from his bear hug. Then he noticed that Alan was wearing pink rubber gloves.

'What's this?' Grassy gasped. 'Don't tell me you've slashed your wrists? Is it an electrocution thing? Are you gassing yourself and electrocuting yourself to make sure? Have you taken an overdose too?'

Grassy held Alan by the shoulders. He adopted his most serious tone.

'Alan. Tell me what you've ingested.'

'A mini steak pie and some roasted veg,' said Alan.

This was not the reply that Grassy had expected. 'Nothing else? Paracetamol? Painkillers? Poison?'

'Have you taken leave of your senses? Explain yourself!'

'You were the one with your head in oven!'

'I was cleaning it!' said Alan, brandishing a pink glove with a bottle of oven cleaner in it. 'Can you smell any gas?'

Grassy took a big sniff. 'No I can't smell any gas.'

'There's a very good reason for that. The oven's electric.'

'I feel like an idiot,' said Grassy.

'You are an idiot,' said Alan.

'Please don't call me an idiot. I'm not having a good day. I decided that my life has no meaning. That I'm useless. That I'm incapable of love. That I'm amoral. That I've been asking all the wrong questions. Then I decided to end it. And then I asked myself: If I'm feeling this bad, I wonder how poor Alan must feel? Then I knew you were in mortal danger.'

'You came to save my life?' said Alan.

'I did,' said Grassy Knoll.

'And you've saved your own.'

'Have I?' said Grassy Knoll.

Alan's face broke out into a magical smile.

'You have.'

Chapter 19 - In the Eaves

Antonia's face was a rather livid shade of red. 'You filthy peeg. You motherfucking son of a whore!' she yelled.

Jamie got the distinct feeling that he wouldn't be having sex that evening.

Earlier on, the Major had come to Jamie's rescue by offering to show him and Antonia the rooms he had available. This enabled Jamie to get them both out from under Anouska's spell. The evening had been heading in a very unusual direction and Jamie wasn't sure whether he'd been involved in the girls' plans at all – in spite of his fantasies.

The minute they saw the room, they knew it was for them: it afforded a view of both roads into the village and offered three different escape routes. The rent was exorbitant. It didn't matter. It was on expenses. It was the room directly above the snug.

But things between them were nowhere near snug. Instead of leaping straight into the sack together, they'd made the fatal mistake of talking to each other first.

Jamie had been braced for an in-depth description of the latest nick-nacks. The fact that Antonia hadn't bought any had somewhat blindsided him. Three pints of Upside Down had further clouded matters.

Jamie's intention had been to describe what an all-round great guy Inspector Witcher was, and how he could be trusted with their secret. It was when he came to describe their side of the bargain that things kicked-off.

'And all we have to do is for me to keep him informed of what's happening on the rig, and you to keep him informed of what's going on in the village.'

'You're turning us into police informants? Grasses? Snouts? Stool pigeons? Snitches? Backstabbers? Liars? Narks? Tell-tales? Eavesdroppers? Gossips? Snidey toads? Squealers? Collaborators? The lowest of the low? Scum?'

'Not informants,' said Jamie, performing a desperate handbrake turn in an attempt to get his hands on her bra straps. 'He just wants us to keep our ears and eyes open and let him know if we see anything unusual. We've to pass on anything notable.'

'I'll give him something notable. I'll give him you – a great, steaming turd.'

Jamie had to admit that, under his tutelage, Antonia's English vocabulary was coming on a treat.

*

Antonia's back was firmly presented toward Jamie when he came to bed. He turned his own back on her and lay, listening to the reassuring murmurs coming from the locals in the snug below. As his eyes adjusted to the dark, he began to pick out the features of their own snug wee room: the sofa wedged behind the skew-whiff door; the unbelievably comfortable armchair wedged in a corner; the ancient dressing table, whose carved roses looked more like carnations, the flower of Spain; the faded mirror, which had seen a few sights; the tiny door in the far corner which led, implausibly, to the enormous bathroom beyond; the two dormer windows which kept the room suitably dim; the ceiling light that had been converted from candles to light-bulbs.

Jamie wondered who else had sat at the dressing table, who else had reflected in the mirror and who else had listened in to conversations below. Perhaps these conversations had developed into fights. Perhaps these conversations were of dark deeds and evil plans. This was certainly a good place to eavesdrop. Jamie quickly found himself able to attune himself to the sounds coming from below.

This was most definitely a good place to hide from Russians.

Jamie lay thinking about Simmo, his dodgy boss. He presumed that Simmo had been unable to track down the lead engineer. He hadn't heard a thing. Simmo hadn't returned his calls. It was worrying. What was even more worrying was the fact that Jamie was supposed to sleep on the site. This suggested that he was on 24 hour call. Alone. Without another engineer i.e. a guy who actually knew what he was doing. Jamie had a grand total of three week's experience on one well, most of that spent dealing with the fallout from the bludgeoned psychopath.

He didn't have a clue what he was doing, he had no other engineer for technical support, and a boss who was very likely a crook. And he was going to have to deal with highly toxic chemicals. In the middle of a village. And then pump those same toxins through the water table.

There may not have been safer places to be, but there were definitely safer things to do.

Antonia was undoubtedly asleep. Her breathing was deep and steady. Jamie was able to make out Anouska's voice. She was a little drunk, getting louder and trying to assert her importance. Grassy Knoll was also drunk and trying to assert his importance. A third voice, unmistakably plummy, was effortlessly important. It belonged to Sir Benjamin Latham MP.

Anouska and Grassy Knoll were trying to get some information out of Sir Benjamin about the owners of Land of Hope & Glory Drilling. The MP was evasive. He claimed not to know, but even through the floorboards Jamie could sense that he was lying. Sir Benjamin was with a friend and when that friend spoke, Jamie realised that Antonia wasn't asleep. She sat bolt upright. Jamie sat bolt upright.

He was speaking heavily accented English – heavily accented in Russian.

Chapter 20 - Jenny

Jennifer sashayed home. Walking was a thing of the past. The Basingstoke makeover had been the best money she had spent. Ever.

They spent two hours perfecting the sashay before they even got to the hair and make-up. By the time they'd finished, her wiggle was getting attention from 18 year-olds. This gave her the confidence boost she so desperately required.

When the make-up girl asked: 'What kind of look do you want? Intelligent and stylish? Alluring? Or full sex siren?'

Jennifer replied: 'Full sex siren. With extra bells and whistles. Fog horns. Gimme everything you've got.'

The make-up girl turned to the clothes stylist: 'Fetch the thigh-length boots.'

The makeover had taken up the entire day. Jennifer needed lessons in everything. It took her about twenty attempts to get her scarlet lipstick applied correctly. There were five different ways that she could arrange her new, casually sexy hairdo. And then there was attitude. Lots and lots of attitude. Boy, did she discover massive untapped reserves of attitude. It was now oozing out of every pore in her amazing girly body.

These weren't just makeover girls. They were psychologists! Motivational heroines. Fifi and Zee. Her sisters! These amazing women had helped her get her female mojo together. Life would never be the same. Jennifer would never be the same. For a start, she was no longer Jennifer. She was Jenny.

Her entrance into the Royal Oak's lounge had been fabulous. Men had gasped! Actually gasped! She had heard it. One guy let out a long, low whistle and muttered something exotic, and probably very filthy, in Spanish. All eyes were on her. She flashed them her insouciant look (15 minutes practice) and eased herself into the snug.

The best bit of all had been watching Anouska's reaction. She'd been lost for words! Anouska! Her face had shock written all over it, shock she couldn't disguise. For a moment she had been, well, very un-Anouska. Un-cool. And then, when she had gathered her senses, delight! Anouska was genuinely delighted at the transformation. And then the delight developed into devilment. Anouska leaned over, kissed her lightly on the lips and then whispered into her ear.

'We'll make a woman of you yet.'

She, Jenny, was the focus of attention. All evening. Nothing could dampen her spirits, not the lovely young drilling couple when they went upstairs to make love, nor the beastly Benjamin and his creepy Russian friend. Both had wanted her. She had power over men. Real power. For the first time. And it felt good.

There was a love letter waiting for her at home.

Jenny wrestled out of the thigh-high boots excitedly, taking care with the fishnet stockings and the chamois mini skirt. Her look had been topped off by a crisp, white linen shirt and her grandmother's pearls. Decorum on top. Filth down below. It all added up, she was told, to an enormous "phwoar" factor. Jenny knew that she still had much to learn. Mistakes would be made. But attitude would see her through. The potential collapse of her rental income no longer worried her. Jenny had made a momentous decision.

She was going to get a job.

For the moment though, there was some serious indulgence in the offing. She poured herself a glass of port and opened some dark, delicious chocolate. She snuggled down into her sofa. Then she opened the letter.

Dearest Jenny, I was stunned by your fierce new look today. Your beauty already took my breath away. Your realisation of your own beauty sent me into paroxysms of pure lust. The gasp that you heard in the tavern was mine.

Gasping, lusting men. It was everything that Jenny wanted. He'd gotten her new name correct too. He'd been spying on her. Jenny ran her tongue over the chocolate as she pressed it into her palate and took a deep cocoa hit. The man was an animal.

I am an animal. I must have you. Every man on planet earth wants you now, but remember that I wanted you first. I saw the real woman hidden in the dowdy clothes. I felt your pure heart. Perhaps you detest me. Perhaps you detest my past. Now there is no me. I have no past. There is only the now of my desire and the future of you, naked, in my arms.

She wasn't so sure whether Hamish could feel her heart. He'd called her a "slapper" the first time they met. The chocolate in her mouth was almost gone now. It was time to take a small draught of port and allow the echo of one flavour to mingle and then be overpowered by the strength of the other. This was ecstasy. Jenny rubbed her feet together in glee. She couldn't wait to be naked in someone's arms.

There is nothing I won't do to prove my love to you. I will leave this crazy business and its exploitative ways. You have brought me a better insanity – the craziness of love. I can't hold back any longer. When I see you now I will come to you and take you in my arms. I will watch over your house, night and day. Oil means nothing to me now. If anything has been fracked, it's my heart. The world means nothing without you in it. Come into my life my darling. I love you forever, Hamish. x

Jenny was impressed by the quality of the stationery. The handwriting wasn't too shoddy either. Hamish was one of those rare children who had been taught penmanship. He had clearly used a fountain pen too. It was a proper love letter, something that could be kept, even if the language still wasn't quite Will Shakespeare. All in all, quite surprising for an oilman. This was one animal that she would have to fight off, which was a shame. Yet there was something naggingly familiar about him which she couldn't put her finger on.

Sipping some more port and popping another piece of dark delight into her mouth, Jenny re-read her lover's latest epistle of adoration and basked in sensuality. Then her thoughts darkened.

There had been a roadblock at the turnoff, three miles from the village, presumably in response to the bomb. The police were now monitoring all the traffic into Foxhole Down. The village was now cut off. They were at the mercy of the oil company. Help wasn't coming. Jenny's imaginary eco-Adonis wasn't coming either. No one was going to be riding in on a white charger. If she was going to get a man, she was going to have to find him herself. He wasn't going to come knocking at her door.

There was a knock at her door.

Jenny felt a thrill of excitement. Perhaps dreams did come true. The knock sounded very gentlemanly and respectful. She skipped across to the hall and opened the door.

In front of her was a squat, Slavic-looking man. The minute she saw him, she knew that she was in trouble. She hadn't seen him before, but he was undoubtedly drillcrew.

Jenny tried closing the door, but the Slav simply stepped inside and forced her backwards. He closed the door behind him. Jenny felt her mouth dry. Her body froze. The man's eyes were bright, dancing at the thought of what he was about to do.

'You are a whore. I like whores.' The voice was indeed Eastern European. 'You may fight, but I know you want me.'

'I want you to leave. I am a woman. I don't need to defend my honour to a psychopath. I want you to leave my house now. I will make a lot of noise. People will come.' Jenny was amazed at her calm amidst the terror.

'Old house. Big walls. No one come.'

He advanced. Jenny retreated, trying desperately to think of potential weapons that were to hand.

The Slav pounced. Jenny couldn't move quickly enough. She was trapped in his arms. She let out a squeal.

The door burst open.

Jenny and the Slav turned to see Hamish looming in the doorframe. His body was taut, ready for action. His face was set and determined.

'You, my friend, are fired,' he said.

The Slav pushed Jenny to Hamish. He picked up a cushion.

Hamish caught Jenny. He stood in front of her, protectively.

The Slav came forward, holding the cushion aloft in one hand. In the other…

'Hamish! He's got a knife!' Jenny yelled.

Hamish leaped forward. He snatched the cushion.

The Slav slashed with his stiletto. Hamish parried with the cushion. The cushion opened, sending feathers across the room.

Hamish punched the Slav, landing an awkward blow to the side of his head. But the Slav was rattled. He slithered out through the door and was gone.

Jenny and Hamish found themselves alone with a ruptured cushion and a mess of feathers.

'Are you cut?' Jenny asked.

Hamish checked. 'No,' he said.

'Would you like a glass of port?'

'I'd like a bottle of port.'

Hamish chuckled. His voice was a little high-pitched. He was more rattled than he was pretending to be. He was a rotten actor.

As Jenny poured the drinks, she noticed that her hand was steady. Hamish didn't seem so bold as he was in his letters. She sashayed across the room and handed him his drink. He downed it in one and handed it back. Jenny pouted archly and sashayed back for a refill. When she proffered him the glass again, he didn't take it. Instead, he slipped inside her arm and drew her to him.

Their noses were almost touching. His eyes were warm and blue and mind-blowing. Jenny knew that this was wrong on so many levels. But her hero had arrived and rescued her.

"Jennifer" would have worried about spilling the port. But "Jenny" threw the glass away and drew her man greedily towards her. She buried her face in his and exchanged a wonderfully wet kiss. Their lovemaking was going to be messy. She didn't care. She was sleeping with the enemy. She didn't care. She barely knew the man. She really really didn't care.

Somehow Hamish had undone the buttons on her blouse. His hand was running up and down her spine, making her draw little gasps. She pulled him back and sucked on his face some more. His aftershave was musky and expensive. He was powerful but tender. Her bra was already undone. She had to decide whether to fuck here or in the bedroom.

She pulled herself clear and strutted over to the front door. She turned the lock. She pulled the curtains closed. She pulled the zip down on her miniskirt.

'Let's fuck here,' she breathed.

Chapter 21 - Morning is Broken

'Here we go again,' said Jamie.

'We are not going anywhere,' replied Antonia, adamantly.

'I suppose we need to check out the Russian.'

'It doesn't matter.'

'Of course it matters. If he's connected to the gangsters, then we move on.'

'I'm sick of this. Constantly on the run.'

'I know darling. I'd hoped we'd be safer here for longer. Russians aren't everywhere. Maybe we need to leave Europe. Go to South America..'

'Fuck South America,' said Antonia. 'I want to live in Europe. I want to live in Spain.'

They were lying in each other's arms, the morning after another passionate night. Life and death trumped domestic squabbles. They'd shagged each other to exhaustion. Now Antonia was exhausted, but in another way.

'We have to confront this,' she continued.

'They'll kill us,' said Jamie.

'I'd rather die on my feet than live on my belly. I'm not bringing a child into a life like this.'

'Perhaps he's nothing to do with gangsters. He was with the local Member of Parliament. Perhaps they'll negotiate. Perhaps…'

'We'll confront the son-of-a-bitch this morning. The politician lives nearby. Anouska will know where he lives.'

Antonia pulled herself up to look Jamie in the eye.

'There's something not right about this job. The whole set-up. It's fucked up.'

*

The Vicar looked at the "Toxic" tanks. They were directly outside his church. These, he presumed, were the carcinogenic chemicals to be used in the fracking. It was an outrageous provocation. It was in defiance of everything he was trying to do in his church. It made his blood boil.

These people would not be content until they had killed, or poisoned, every living thing on the planet. Where were their souls? But more importantly the vicar thought: where was his soul?

The Vicar noted that he had lost his lodger to the arms of a dusky Spanish beauty. It also appeared that Jennifer had become a fallen woman.

The Vicar surveyed his parish, such as it was. He needed a drink.

*

Jenny woke up with a man! Ok, so life had left him a little crumpled and the worse for wear, but there he was! He felt warm! He smelled great! He was all hers! She was all his!

Jenny wondered in which of the million thrilling directions their relationship would head. Walks in the woods. Snuggling up in front of the fire. Holding hands at sunset. What would they do next?

She knew what she would do next: she would feed him.

*

Jamie was up the down, looking down on Foxhole Down. He was trying to get a signal to talk to Simmo.

'Hi Simmo, it's Jamie. I have a few concerns about the job. We're about to start drilling and there's no water, no chemicals and nowhere to put the rock cuttings. The other engineer hasn't shown up.'

'There's some bad news about the other engineer.' Simmo sounded as if he was still in bed. Jamie could hear a woman stirring in the background. 'His bender got a bit out of hand. There was an unpaid restaurant bill. Then things went downhill. There was an incident with a transvestite policeman and a Thai tourist. He seems to have exposed himself. Then he resisted arrest. He was found with some drugs on him too. I'm trying to track him down. Are you any good on London prisons?'

'There was no other engineer,' Jamie shouted. 'My cabin only has one bedroom in it. It's my second trip. I don't have a clue what I'm doing. I'm supposed to provide 24 hour cover. I've no chemicals and we're going to begin drilling this afternoon. Help!'

Jamie's voice echoed uselessly into the trees, startling a lone wood pigeon.

Simmo put on his kindliest voice. 'Don't worry. There's a truck coming with some chemicals. And if you need help, I'm always on the end of the line.'

Jamie couldn't help but think of Gray, the useless engineer he'd worked with offshore. He also had a tendency to drop Jamie right in it.

'You won't need any chemicals, Simmo continued. 'Drilling top hole is easy. All you need is a couple of viscous sweeps. Go to the supermarket. Chuck some custard powder in. In fact, all you really need is water.'

'We don't have any water either!' Jamie shrieked.

'Ah,' said Simmo. 'I'm working on that. Frank's at the reservoir right now, sucking some up.'

'Who's Frank?'

'He's our tanker driver. And chemical delivery guy. He'll have a couple of sacks for you in his cabin.'

'You don't suck water out a reservoir. It's another scam, isn't it Simmo?'

'Well...'

'How much are you charging for this water?'

'Ah...'

'Who owns the tanker?'

'You see...'

'How much are you charging for the tanker? How much are you charging for Frank? Does Frank know how much you're charging? Hold on a minute: how much are you charging for me?'

Simmo adopted his most innocent voice. 'There's no need for you to concern yourself about any of this.'

'I hate you!' Jamie yelled.

The wood pigeon, who had returned, took it personally and flew off again.

'Everything to do with Saint Francis of Assisi Drilling Fluids is a scam, isn't it?'

Simmo was silent.

'Here's one more scam for you,' said Jamie. 'My day rate has just gone up to fifteen hundred quid a day. And I'm going to give you my bank details. And you're going to transfer ten thousand pounds into my account. And if it's not there by this time tomorrow, I'm walking off the job. And I'll set Rooster and his drillcrew on you – and they're not nice.

*

Antonia breezed in to Anouska's lovely rectory. She didn't knock.

Anouska was sitting on the paint-spattered floor of her front room, studying a canvas.

'I was hoping you'd come,' said Anouska.

'How could I stay away?' said Antonia, with a shrug.

Anouska flicked her eyes towards the canvas. What do you think?

Antonia's face broke into a warm smile. Anouska was delighted to see such a reaction to one of her works.

'It's chaotic,' said Antonia. 'But very female. It is totally woman.'

Anouska raised her hand. Antonia grasped it firmly and raised Anouska to her feet. By happy coincidence, this also drew Anouska into her arms. They slipped seamlessly into a kiss - tender, sensual and spine-tingling.

When they broke, they realised that they were both breathing heavily. Anouska smiled. Antonia giggled.

'I feel like I'm at the beginning of a fabulous adventure,' Antonia breathed. 'I haven't stopped thinking about you since I first saw you.'

'You've been.. dominating my thoughts too.' Anouska whispered into Antonia's ear. 'I've been in a very erotic state of anticipation. The dam's about to burst. I am going to paint you. But I'm going to enjoy you first.'

Antonia drew Anouska's head to hers. She ran her tongue along Anouska's top lip and stared deeply into her eyes.

'I think we're going to be very bad for one another.'

*

'We're in trouble,' said Jamie.

'We sure are,' said Rooster.

'No chems. No water. No drilling,' said Jamie.

'No bordellos. No whores. No drilling,' said Rooster.

'I've tried everything,' said Alan, plaintively.

'Using his extensive contact book,' said Rooster, caustically.

They were in Rooster's office.

'I've got some bad news about St. Francis of Assisi Drilling Fluids,' said Jamie.

'What about St. Francis of Assisi Drilling Fluids?' said Rooster.

'St Francis of Assisi Drilling Fluids is basically a compulsive liar armed with a telephone.'

'Son, the entire oil industry is a compulsive liar and a telephone.'

'I just wanted you to know that I'm doing my best,' said Jamie.

'I know that you're doing your best, son,' said Rooster. 'You've got "sucker" written all over you.'

'And what are you doing?' Jamie asked.

'As little harm as humanly possible,' said Rooster. 'Which is to say: a whole lot more harm than is necessary.'

Rooster looked out of his window. It offered him the best view he could have asked for. It was a view of his derrick. Things should have been moving. Nothing was moving.

'Stop worrying, Jamie. We'll get water from somewhere. We can drill top hole with that. It's the lack of a cat house that concerns me more. We need a Goddamn miracle.'

'Perhaps the Vicar could help with that,' said Jamie.

Rooster's eyes lit up. Jamie could sense what he was thinking. 'No!' he shouted. 'You're not using the church as some house of ill-repute.'

'You idiot!' said Rooster. 'I'm not a heathen. I was thinking about the blessing! Assemble the crew. Get the Vicar's ass over here. Let's get God on the hydrocarbon case. He's never let us down before.'

Jamie paused on his way out of the door. 'I was thinking about a, em, location for the girls. What about Fletcher's house?'

'Him?' said Rooster. 'He's my new Head of Security.'

'He's the local crook,' said Alan.

'I know. As Head of Security he's liable to steal far less from us.'

Rooster smiled ruefully.

'But I like your thinking, kid. It's given me an idea. I know the perfect place for our bordello.'

The colour left Alan's face. 'You're not using my house.'

Rooster grinned. 'Oh it's far worse than that.'

Chapter 22 - Bless Me Father, I'm About to Sin

The crew had gathered in its entirety. They might have been as bent as a bishop's crook, but they were as superstitious as hell too.

Jamie led the Vicar in. The crew parted like the Red Sea. Jamie had only just got to the Vicar in the nick of time, just as he was beginning his sixth pint of Upside Down.

The Vicar was unshaven. His hair was unkempt. He was unsteady on his feet. He was a disgrace to the cloth. The crew loved it.

There was spontaneous applause. There were various shouts.

'Go Padre!'

'Bless us father!'

'We love you Vicar, you got cojones!'

'Punch the Toolpusher again!'

'Looks like we got our own whisky priest!'

A man grabbed his arm. 'Padre, will you hear my confession? I have a lot on my chest.'

'Of course my son,' said the Vicar, trying to focus.

'I hope you've got a large space in your diary,' said Jamie. 'It won't be a quick one.'

'Why you…' The man grabbed Jamie. A scuffle ensued. The Vicar got knocked over.

There was a gasp. It was a bad omen.

As Jamie picked the Vicar up, the man backed off. He was then whacked on the head with a hard hat. Rooster took control of the situation.

'The Vicar's doing his own little seismic survey. Is there oil, Vicar?'

The Vicar nodded vigorously. There was a cheer. The Vicar dusted himself off and was helped onto a small podium made up of stacked wooden pallets. As he rose above the crowd, the cheering grew. Having milked it for some moments – with an impudent smile on his face – the Vicar raised his arms to quieten the crowd.

'Dearly beloved,' the Vicar began, 'we stand here, united in Christ, penitent before God, as sinners.'

A cheer: sinning went down well with this mob.

'You lot might not be to everybody's taste, but let me tell you right now: if Jesus was here, you'd be exactly the kind of guys he'd be hanging about with.'

A bigger cheer: this went down really well.

'Jesus liked so-called scumbags. Shepherds. Prostitutes.'

Big cheer for prostitutes.

'He knew who the salt of the earth were.'

Big cheer: the drillcrew knew exactly who the salt of the earth were.

'And who did he crack up at? When was the one time Jesus lost his temper? That's right; the moneylenders at the Temple. Jesus hated bankers. It's in the Book. It's official. Bankers are bastards.'

Huge cheer.

'It's not your fault the world's fixed. You haven't become whoring, thieving cut-throats as a lifestyle choice, have you?'

'No!' they shouted, although most of them had.

'I do not hold you personally responsible for what is going on here. I blame capitalism. Or the shoddy kleptocracy that passes for it. Although that's a technical matter that I won't go into here. Not only have you lot been dealt a bad hand, the game's been rigged and the cards are stacked against you. In this scam, the dealer always wins.'

Applause: he'd lost them for a moment, but had got them back.

'Get a move-on, Vicar.' Rooster spoke out of the corner of his mouth. 'The oil's been down there 100 million years. We don't have another 100 million.'

'My point precisely,' the Vicar slurred. 'Gentlemen, I have been requested to get a move-on and I will. Because, let's face it, we don't want to turn this into another crucifixion. Although personally speaking, I think that the centurion wanted to get a move-on there as well.'

'The blessing, Vicar!' Rooster hissed.

'Let us bow our heads for the blessing and the Holy Water, which isn't strictly a Church of England thing, but I'm willing to put a show on for the Catholics amongst you. Couldn't organise incense at short notice. Holy water.'

The Vicar held up what looked like a bottle of Brown Ale. He received a smattering of applause. Heads were bowed.

'Dearly Beloved. We are gathered here today to fuck the planet up. Grant us success in this venture. With no man or woman hurt or injured. No fatalities. No spills. No poisoning of the water table. No botched cement jobs. No stuck pipe. No losses of drilling fluid. And a jolly good Rate of Penetration.'

There was sincere applause for this. The Vicar had done his research.

'Let us give thanks to the Almighty who has made this possible: that is to say, the US Federal Reserve, whose hot money, hot off the printing presses is financing this and lots of other shenanigans. May our Lord forgive the massive capital misallocation that is going on, the artificially low Bond Yields that will come back to bite us on the behind. May the collapse of the monetary system not leave too many of us destroyed and Lord, grant us the wisdom to invest in real assets, lest we get caught with our financial trousers down. And may we all have some gold in our portfolio, say 10%, as insurance and grant us all enough ready cash to see us through the coming catastrophe, because financial gravity cannot be defied forever. May no one get run off and may everyone come to an understanding of Gaia, Mother Earth, Your creation, who sustains us all. May God forgive us our trespasses on the way to the payzone. And I'm sorry for the mud bombs. But I'm not sorry about punching your boss. He was asking for it.'

This got the biggest cheer of the day.

'In summary, Dear Lord. Bless the planet. Bless this wayward flock. Stuff the money men. Fuck the bankers. And send everyone home with wallets full of dollars and hearts full of Jesus.'

'Amen,' said Rooster.

'Amen!' said the drillcrew.

'Amen!' shouted the Vicar. He tried to bless the congregation with the Holy Water, but the beer bottle flew out of his hand, hit the Toolpusher square between the eyes and knocked him clean out.

This was taken as a good omen.

Chapter 23 - The Hit

When Jamie set eyes on Antonia, his heart soared. Her hair was slightly unkempt. There was a little colour, almost a glow, about her face. A smile was playing on her lips. She was utterly alive. How beautiful she looked.

'Darling you look so wonderful,' Jamie said. 'It's as if you've found some kind of inner peace.'

Antonia nodded. 'I've been making love to Anouska,' she said.

'What??!!' Jamie shrieked.

Another woodpigeon fled in fright. It was becoming a habit. They were in a clearing in the ancient wood, on their way to see a conservative MP and a Russian gangster.

'You're having an affair?' Jamie was slack jawed.

'Don't get ahead of yourself,' said Antonia. 'I only put my clothes back on ten minutes ago. For the moment it's just sex.'

'And where does that leave us?' Jamie was almost whimpering.

'In an ancient wood, on our way to see a conservative MP and a Russian gangster.'

'You've been unfaithful to me.'

'You had an affair first.'

'No I didn't.'

'Yes you did. You had Anouska last night. With your eyes!'

Jamie spluttered. 'It's not the same thing at all,' he said.

'Yes, it's far worse. You were thinking about a threesome. You disgust me.'

Jamie was silent. Gobsmacked.

'And now you seek to deny me this fantastic experience.'

Jamie's jaw moved, but nothing came out.

'You think that the beauty of women and the pleasures of their flesh are things that only men should enjoy. Not only do you create this nightmare world, you seek to control the one female part of it. I enjoyed her. And knowing that you will never touch her made the ecstasy twice as great.'

Jamie's opening and closing mouth was now making him look like a rather lanky fish.

'What is this?' Antonia held up her left hand.

Jamie, suspecting that this was a trick question, said nothing.

'Do you see a ring on it? No! So how dare you try to control me?'

'I had no idea that marriage was an issue,' said Jamie.

'You should put that on your tombstone: "I had no idea". Your life in four words.'

Jamie walked along, unsteadily, wondering why he was feeling guilty about letting Antonia down rather than being outraged at her infidelity.

'When we go into the house, let me do all the talking,' said Antonia. 'You are in no state to say anything coherent.'

Jamie wasn't about to argue.

*

Vladimir Rokossovsky installed himself into Benjamin Latham's unfeasibly comfortable armchair and drank his unfeasibly awful tea.

The English were shit at tea.

The English, Vladimir Rokossovsky felt, were shit at lots of things. They were certainly shit at making deals. The deal that he had done with Benjamin was too good to be true. He couldn't possibly lose out of it. The fact that it was also going to despoil a beautiful little corner of England was the cherry on the icing on the cake.

Lots of land in Russia was despoiled. But then again, there was an awful lot of land in Russia to despoil. It felt good to be spreading the shit around. Right on Benjamin's doorstep too. So long as they kept London intact, they could lay waste to the entire island as far as Vladimir was concerned.

'This is a pretty little dacha you have for yourself,' Vladimir said.

'Indeed,' said Benjamin, sipping his delicious tea. 'Terribly handy for London, you know – my club, the City, the fabulous eateries, and the raunchy ladies stashed in Bayswater apartments.'

Benjamin tapped the side of his nose in a confidential manner. His wife was in Dorset with her sister.

'And it's convenient for Parliament too,' Benjamin added. 'Talking of which, how are things between you and Mr Putin?'

'He likes to keep us dancing. The secret is to keep close to a chair for when he makes the music stop. Unfortunately, Russian politics isn't as corrupt as British politics.'

Benjamin almost choked on his jam roly-poly. 'I beg your pardon?'

Vladimir looked at the MP with an almost pained expression. 'Don't get all Downton Abbey with me, my friend. You write the laws that steal from your people in plain sight. You have been doing it for hundreds of years. In Russia, I have to be a crook to make money.'

'Oh I say,' said Benjamin Latham.

'Don't get me wrong, I respect that,' said Vladimir Rokossovsky. 'We had a revolution. The thieves changed. You still have the same thieves. I congratulate you. Long may your scam continue.'

Vladimir raised a teacup in salute. The doorbell rang. Benjamin returned with Jamie and Antonia. Jamie took a tea. Antonia refused a coffee.

'The English are shit at coffee,' said Antonia.

Vladimir nodded triumphantly. 'I think we are going to get along,' he said, taking in an eyeful of Antonia.

Jamie went up to Vladimir. 'Don't even think about it, sunshine.'

'Do you know who I am?' said Vladimir.

'I already have a death sentence hanging over me. You can't kill me twice. Besides, she prefers women. Artistic women.'

'Now chaps,' said Benjamin, 'I always feel that it's best policy to assume that we are being listened to. By the CSA.'

'The Child Support Agency?' said Jamie.

'No, the American lot.'

'The NSA,' said Antonia.

'That's the National Sheep Association,' said Benjamin.

'Why would they be listening in?' said Vladimir.

'Let us assume,' said Benjamin, 'that the CIA are listening in to everything we say. There is therefore no need to talk about killing or anything horrible like that. And I wouldn't know what you were talking about anyway.'

'Before we begin,' said Jamie, 'I want to make it clear that it is Britain that is shit at coffee. I want Scotland included.'

No one argued.

'We have not come here by accident,' Antonia began. 'And we don't think that you have come here by accident either.'

Vladimir Rokossovsky smiled enigmatically.

'If I were to mention sixty million dollars' worth of cocaine which went missing on a North Sea oil rig, would that ring any bells?'

'The Kremlin has less bells than are ringing in my head just now.'

'Good,' Antonia smiled. 'You appreciate that we were not the custodians of these drugs? That Jamie destroyed them by mistake? That the man truly responsible was murdered? His son also?'

'And you appreciate that me and my partners do not like to be made to look like fools. And you appreciate that when we lose large sums of money that it makes us look weak in the minds of our enemies? And you appreciate that being an idiot is no excuse in our world?'

'I am a girl who appreciates a lot. But we stumbled into your world.'

Vladimir held his hands up. 'It is,' he said, 'our world. You should have stayed out of it.'

'What does killing us achieve?'

'It will be a Public Relations victory for us.'

'I'm to die for a PR stunt!' said Jamie.

'It will be quick,' said the Russian. 'Spectacular, but quick.'

Jamie and Antonia exchanged a wary glance.

'Spectacular?' said Jamie.

'We want to make a big splash. In the Russian press. It's important to let all the players know that we have killed the idiot who made us look like idiots.'

'Are you telling me that it's really only Jamie that you need to kill?' said Antonia.

'You, my dear, could make it up to us in other ways,' smarmed the Russian.

'I'm an open-minded girl,' Antonia shrugged.

'Surely there is a more civilised way around this?' squeaked Jamie.

Antonia beamed a radiant smile at him.

'Darling, you're dumped.'

Benjamin Latham MP, and Vladimir Rokossovsky Russian gangster, roared with laughter. They adored betrayal.

Jamie stood up and gestured. 'You adulterous lesbian Spanish cow!'

This made Benjamin and Vladimir worse. They were like sniggering schoolboys.

'Don't be a drama queen,' said Antonia. 'Sit down and finish your tea.'

'While you lot plot my murder?' said Jamie. 'And the resultant publicity campaign?'

'Why not? We'd appreciate your input,' Vladimir laughed.

Jamie walked calmly to the French door, in an attempt to regain some dignity. 'If you don't mind, I'll select the traditional option in these circumstances: I'll flee for my life.'

Vladimir stopped laughing.

'You won't make it out of the woods.'

Jamie shuffled back to the sofa and sat down.

Antonia patted him on the knee.

'Thanks,' said Jamie. 'That makes my spectacular murder all the more bearable. I can't imagine why I was so upset.'

Vladimir leaned forward in his chair. 'You mentioned lesbianism?'

'Yes,' said Jamie. 'I should have realised that the writing was on the wall. She and Anouska have been getting into each other's knickers.'

'It was very pleasurable,' Antonia beamed.

'I bet it was,' said Benjamin. 'Did you film anything?'

'Not yet,' said Antonia, coyly.

'If you were to produce such a movie, that would go a long way to forgive your indiscretions,' said Vladimir.

'Now that I am free, anything is possible. I think she wants to paint me nude. I would expect that we would be making love during that. A film would almost be a work of art in itself. I would hope that it would grant me total forgiveness.'

'Forgive me for being a greedy man, but I would like to fuck you too. Both of you.'

'We'll see.' Antonia nibbled her fingers seductively.

'I don't want to be a bore,' said Jamie, 'but I can't help thinking about this sudden spectacular murder of mine.'

'Don't be vulgar,' said Benjamin.

'Have you no taste?' said Antonia.

'Well I'm sorry!' Jamie yelled. 'Are we talking about a bullet in the head in central London, or what?'

'I was thinking along the lines of a car-bomb in a supermarket car park,' said Vladimir.

'I'm not dying in a supermarket car park!

'Don't worry,' said Benjamin, 'it won't be anywhere horrid like Lidl or Aldi. We'll give you a classy send-off in Waitrose.'

'I don't want to be blown to smithereens,' Jamie moaned.

'Behave!' said Antonia testily.

'On the other hand, I feel a bomb could be a touch messy,' said Benjamin. 'If others got injured..'

'Okay, so a bomb in the middle of nowhere,' said Vladimir.

'How about his bullet-riddled body being found hanging from a London landmark?' ventured Antonia.

'That would get massive publicity,' said Benjamin.

'I like it,' said Vladimir.

'You really are a complete and utter cow,' said Jamie.

'What are you going to do, tell your policeman friend?' Antonia turned to Vladimir. 'He's a police informant.'

'The lowest of the low,' said Benjamin Latham MP.

'The best thing to do with rats is shoot them,' said Vladimir.

'Or poison them,' said Antonia.

Vladimir's eyebrows shot up. 'I like the sound of that.'

'Of course,' said Jamie. 'I could fall into my soup while lunching with President Putin. Or the President of the United States. Or the Pope. Any high profile meal would generate a ton of publicity. Or maybe a sky-diving accident. In Red Square.'

'I think you should come to Russia to die,' said Vladimir.

'It's as good a place as any,' said Jamie cheerfully. Mentally, he had moved to the strange, giddy region that existed beyond panic.

'I think it's best if I take Jamie back to the pub,' said Antonia solicitously.

'Don't worry,' said Vladimir to Jamie. 'We need you to help drill the well. Once that's finished, we'll come to an agreement that satisfies us all.'

'I can't wait to hear what that is,' said Jamie. 'Public beheading at the Tower of London? Defenestration in Prague? A catapult into the Grand Canyon?'

Antonia led him away by the arm. 'I will see you both soon, gentlemen. I know that Anouska is looking forward to it. You should come tomorrow. She has an art dealer coming to look at some of her canvases. It should be thrilling.'

Back in the woods, Jamie ran around, flapping his arms, trying to scare as many woodpigeons as possible.

'Whee!' said Jamie.

'Calm down and stop being so stupid,' Antonia hissed.

'I'm dumped. I'm dead. I don't care!'

Jamie skipped gaily through the trees. 'Of all the fracking jobs, on all the village greens in the world, he has to walk into ours.

What were the odds?'

'They were never going to go away, Jamie. We had to face them some time. Better to do it now.'

'Why die tomorrow when you can die today?' said Jamie, dancing alongside Antonia.

Antonia grabbed Jamie by the arm. 'If you didn't notice, I just saved one of our lives. All I have to do now is save your sorry ass. Not that you deserve it.'

Jamie was indignant. 'You have signed my death warrant and slept with another woman!'

'You are so ungrateful.'

Chapter 24 - Well Well Well

They broke ground at 1.15 pm, shortly after the ambulance left.

Jamie got his water deliveries, just in time, from Frank, who drove a lovely silver tanker.

'That were a close thing,' said Frank. 'Can't go back to that reservoir. People have got all antsy about drinking water what with Osama Bin Whatsit. God knows where the next load will come from. Make sure you order well in advance. There's a feller in Dorset what's got some water he wants rid of. Might have a bit of cow piss in it. Good enough for your purposes.'

This didn't fill Jamie with optimism.

His ingratitude with Antonia had, apparently, been the final straw. After a brief glimmer of hope, he was well-and-truly dumped. He'd had to move his things out of the pub and into his small and filthy cabin.

'I need you to do one important thing,' Antonia had said. 'I want all the money that's in the bank.'

'That's three-quarters of a million pounds,' said Jamie.

'Then give it to me.'

'What's it for?'

'I can't have it in a bank. They'll take it. I need to convert it into something valuable.'

'Do I get to keep any of it?'

'If you survive.'

'What if I refuse to do it?'

'I'll have Vladimir kill you sooner rather than later.'

Jamie was definitely dumped. Definitely.

The ambulance took away a casual stabbing casualty. The motivation was unclear, but the solution was glaringly obvious.

'We need whores and we need them now,' said Rooster.

"Brothel Fixtures & Fittings" wasn't something that Alan had Googled before, but he was gamely trying to furnish a couple of rooms from scratch.

'Make sure you get a Jacuzzi,' said Rooster.

'Indoor or outdoor?' said Alan.

'Inflatable,' said Rooster. 'They can stick it where the hell they like.'

Hamish, as the fixer, was ordered to fix the whore drought.

'Let's face it, as far as whores are concerned, Alan's about as much use as tits on a bull,' said Rooster.

'I'll take that as a compliment,' said Alan, tartly.

'What sort of whores are you looking for?' said Hamish.

'Most of the boys are Latinos of some description,' said Rooster. 'Go Spanish-themed. I don't want any trafficked girls. Just good, hard-working girls. Self-employed types.'

'Six ought to keep us going. And keep them going,' said Hamish. 'Any less and they bitch amongst themselves. Any more and they bitch among themselves.'

Hamish immediately got to the heart of the matter: he went to see Fletcher, who was at the gate, wearing a uniform that he'd already managed to dishevel.

Hamish handed Fletcher a list. 'This is what's arriving today: 120 feet of conductor pipe; 1000 feet of drill pipe; 3 cuttings skips; 2 drill bits; 2 loads of cementing chemicals; and one load of brothel fixtures and fittings.'

'I always said it was what the village needed,' said Fletcher, leering and grinning. It was the best news ever.

'You look like a man of the world,' said Hamish, eyeing Fletcher doubtfully. 'Where am I likely to find six working girls with a Spanish flavour?'

'Go down the docks at Portsmouth,' said Fletcher. 'I'll come with you and run an eye over them.'

'I know exactly what kind of eye you'll be running over them,' said Hamish. 'But I need something more upmarket than dock girls.'

'There's all sorts around Gatwick,' said Fletcher eagerly. 'I can help.'

'I don't think so,' said Hamish dourly.

'I know you from somewhere,' said Fletcher. 'I've definitely seen you before. When I remember, it'll be trouble for you.' Fletcher gave his toothy-toothless smile.

Hamish walked away. He'd consult with his contact about the girls. Sometimes he felt that he was the only person who knew what was really going on.

*

The drilling, although brief, brought some relief to Jamie. Having something to do cleared his head. They began drilling with fresh water but once it had been round the system a couple of times, it became quite muddy. Jamie assumed that that was the reason why drilling fluid was called "mud".

It wasn't rocket science.

By eight in the evening, they'd drilled enough to keep Rooster happy. He called TD, which was the nickname for the end of the section. It had been so long since Jamie's one and only drilling experience that he felt as if he was starting from scratch. Still, thinking about drilling and mud kept his mind off imminent assassination.

'Go get Upside Down,' said Rooster. 'The boys will run conductor pipe tonight. The cementer will mix some of his chemicals and then get some sleep. We'll cement this bitch in the morning.'

Sitting in the pub with a pint and a delicious steak was a great way to round off a day's drilling, Jamie thought. Land jobs were definitely better than the North Sea.

'Have you got anything for me?' It was Inspector Witcher, who slid onto a stool beside Jamie.

'Have I got something for you!' Jamie trilled. 'Part of the finance for this is coming from the Russian Mafia.'

At this, Grassy Knoll came over and joined them.

'Grassy Knoll, compulsive conspiracy theorist,' said Grassy Knoll, offering his hand.

'Inspector Witcher, sworn enemy of all conspiracies,' said Inspector Witcher, receiving it.

'Here's the bombshell,' said Jamie. 'I'm to be killed.'

Neither Grassy nor Witcher batted an eyelid.

'I take it,' said Witcher, 'that this is in revenge for you inadvertently destroying forty million quid's worth of their cocaine?'

'Yes.'

'You can hardly blame them.'

'Aren't you going to do something?'

'Aren't you?'

'Like what?'

'Like run away?'

'What kind of a reaction is that from the police?' said Jamie. 'I'm disgusted at you.'

'We can't arrest someone until a crime has been committed,' said Witcher.

'Can't you put me on the Witness Protection Programme?'

'What have you witnessed?'

'Well, nothing.'

'Then we can't put you on the Witness Protection Programme.'

'Let's go back to what you were saying about the Russian Mafia,' said Grassy Knoll.

Jamie explained as best he could about Vladimir and Benjamin, his betrayal by Antonia and her passionate affair with Anouska. Both men listened intently.

'This is tricky,' said Witcher. 'We're dealing with powerful forces.'

'They could be Illuminati,' said Grassy Knoll. 'Did either of them mention Land of Hope and Glory Drilling? Silent partners? Tax havens?'

'You should have been an Inspector,' said Witcher. 'You're a natural.'

Grassy Knoll's eyes sparkled. 'That's the nicest thing anyone's ever said to me.'

The Vicar collapsed into their midst. He was very drunk.

'I'm sorry to hear that you're to be killed,' he said. 'You don't deserve it, but neither did Jesus. I'd happily take your place if I could. The world is a terrible place and we are better off out of it. I have lived a long and disreputable life. I worshipped the golden calf when I should have been doing the Lord's work among thieves and prostitutes.'

'I wouldn't give up on that dream,' said Jamie. 'You may be about to get your chance.'

'You're a disgrace,' said Grassy Knoll. 'You're turning into a whisky priest.'

'Whisky Vicar,' the Vicar corrected. 'The Church of England could drink the Catholics under the table.'

The Vicar fell under the table.

'I can't help but feel that our institutions are failing us,' said Jamie. He turned to Witcher. 'Are you really telling me that you can't help me until I've been attacked?'

'I'd love to help,' said Witcher. 'But there's been budget cuts.'

Jamie gulped his Upside Down desperately. 'I'm to die for budget cuts?'

Chapter 25 - The Whorehouse

Alan approached his curtains with trepidation. It had been another restless night. Ordering the goods to kit out a brothel hadn't been the best way to settle his nerves. The revenge of the one-legged men still loomed large. He had never expected to open his curtains to anything other than a village green, neglected or otherwise. The oil rig was a shocking sight – a daily reminder of a world gone completely mad. It reminded Alan of the last book he had read, as a teenage boy. Frodo Baggins had returned to find his beloved Shire despoiled by Sharkey and his henchmen. Fortunately the gangsters were routed and the Shire restored by magical elven dust.

Would that Alan's own beloved world could be so easily restored. Still, he had a very bad feeling about what he was about to confront.

Alan was not disappointed. Or rather, he was disappointed in a way that he could not have possibly imagined. No one had told him exactly where the new whorehouse was going to be. Now it was standing right in front of him.

The new whorehouse was the old cricket pavilion.

*

When Alan came to, he was sitting at his kitchen table with a cup of tea in front of him. He went back to his front window just to make sure. Yes, they'd moved the boundary fence so that the pavilion was now outside the drilling package. They'd also put a gate in the fence to provide easy access. This was just as well, because it was shift changeover and it looked like the entire night shift were paying a visit. And there, by the main door, where he used to lay out a travelling rug for picnics, was the outdoor Jacuzzi. And there, in the outdoor Jacuzzi, were two naked men and two naked women. And the naked women were bobbing up and down. It was too awful to think about.

'I'll jolly well phone the police,' Alan found himself saying. 'If that's not worth an Anti-Social Behaviour Order, nothing is.'

But his landline rang first. It was Rooster. 'Al, we're getting some heat about this God-damn whorehouse. I've squared things up with the cops. If anyone phones to complain, they're getting told that they'll be visited by a community liaison officer.'

'Finally, some sanity,' said Alan.

'You're the community liaison officer.'

'I beg your pardon?'

'Inspector Witcher will give you a list of names and addresses. I'll give you a bag of money. I want you to go round the houses and smooth things over. Explain that it's not really a whorehouse. The girls are on the payroll as "rig hostesses". What they do to the boys is entirely up to them.'

'I saw two of them just now. They were in the Jacuzzi. They were bobbing up and down.'

'There's worse things happen in the world, Al. Look on the bright side, at least the building is less likely to get damaged.'

'Did you have to paint it pink?'

'The boys wanted a neon sign. I spared you that, at least.'

'It's a cricket pavilion,' Alan wailed. 'It's designed for people to have cups of tea and cucumber sandwiches. Gentle conversations about their knock, or a catch in the slips. I'm torturing myself imagining what's going on in there. It's a desecration.'

'As far as these payoffs go,' said Rooster. 'No more than two hundred pounds per household.' He hung up.

So Alan was now a bag man for a brothel. He knew that things were only going to get worse.

Chapter 26 - Art for Art's Sake

It was one of the most bizarre mornings of Benjamin Latham MP's life - or Vladimir Rokossovsky's, for that matter – and he'd had an incredibly bizarre life.

The men were in bohemian heaven.

The men were in Anouska's studio. They were watching Anouska paint Antonia in the nude. Antonia was naked and reclining on a velvet chaise longue with a Persian-patterned silk sheet draped artfully over her body. Anouska was also naked, standing behind her canvas, occasionally giving the men sensational flashes of her immaculate body.

Occasionally, Anouska would declare a break and she and Antonia would snog furiously for a couple of minutes. It was an incredible turn-on for the men, who were joyously sipping some 2009 Trotanoy.

The wine was an amazing vintage. The women were an amazing vintage.

The most bizarre thing of all though, was Jasper Jones, Anouska's art dealer. Marching around the house, Jasper was shrieking with delight at each new canvas he discovered. He would shout through a description of the artwork – and a price.

Jasper was also quite naked.

'Darlings,' he announced, stomping back into the studio, 'the only thing that is worthwhile about art is that which can't be explained.' Jasper took a deep breath and held his hands up. 'And I can't explain any of this!' he shouted. 'IT'S FANTASTIC !!!'

'Jasper,' Vladimir observed, 'you have a very small willy.'

Anouska arched a paint-spattered eyebrow at Vladimir.

'Oh never mind that,' said Jasper, dismissing his own appendage. 'I'm going to sell these. FOR A FORTUNE !!!'

These last three words made Vladimir perk up.

'Don't even think about stealing one,' said Anouska.

'Anouska, give me a break. I am an art lover. I want to buy. I am sure we could negotiate a price.'

Anouska stuck a brush in her mouth. 'We could negotiate my boot up your arse,' she said. 'You can bid with everybody else.'

'I'm sure we can come to an arrangement,' Jasper whispered.

'Jasper,' Anouska shouted, 'are you an expert on old art?'

'Old art?' said Jasper incredulously. 'Old art? My darling, do you mean: Do I know a Matisse from a Modigliani? A Poussin from a Picasso? A Cezanne from a Seurat? Do I wield a magnifying glass in my professional life? Do I resort to the use of x-ray equipment? Am I au-fait with carbon-dating and craquelure? Yes, yes, yes, yes, yes, yes and yes!' Jasper paraded to Antonia's side. 'Why do you ask?'

'I'm getting in to the market myself. I may need to check the provenance.'

'Then look no further,' said Jasper.

Antonia drew herself close and stroked Anouska's hair.

'Not now, Antonia,' said Anouska sternly.

Antonia pouted.

'Mr Rokossovsky, are you a lover of art?' Anouska asked coyly.

'I am a lover of beauty. I am a lover of money. And I am a lover of dishonesty,' Vladimir grinned.

'And are you familiar with the paintings at the Hermitage in St. Petersburg?'

'The official collection, or the unofficial one?' said Vladimir.

'They haven't got a load of loot from World War 2 have they?' said Benjamin, himself an admirer of the underhand.

'The Hermitage collection is nothing but loot,' said Vladimir. Mainly confiscated during the Revolution. For sure we have some pieces taken from the Germans, who took it from the Jews. It was legitimately paid for.'

'Oh come on,' Benjamin laughed.

'It was paid for with the blood of twenty million Russians.'

Vladimir very suddenly turned very serious.

'If there are any rich bastards who think that they have a legitimate claim to this art, let them come and fight us for it.'

Antonia raised a glass. 'I agree.'

'All property is theft my dear Benjamin,' said Vladimir.

'I'd forgotten how dyed-in-the-wool you communists were,' said Benjamin.

Anouska slipped on a denim shirt and did up a single button. She moved sexily amongst the men.

'Remember civilisation?' she said.

'Vaguely,' said Benjamin off-handedly.

'The Hermitage is a world-renowned centre of a thing once known as civilisation. They care for those works and they make them available to everyone. The Hermitage is a beacon of hope in a darkening world,' said Vladimir sombrely.

Anouska picked up the bottle of Trotanoy and leaned against the mantel. She swigged gratefully, her breasts bursting out of the shirt and her labia available for all to see beneath her stylishly-quiffed pubic hair.

'What use is Art on the wall of a rich cunt?' she said.

Chapter 27 - Cementing Relationships

Once the conductor pipe had been run into the hole that they had drilled, it required to be cemented into position. This turned out to be a little bit trickier than Jamie had anticipated.

'We need trucks?' he said. 'It was so much easier in the North Sea. So long as there was no oil involved, everything went over the side.'

'Son, if you can show me a side to throw excess cement over, I'll put it there,' said Rooster. 'Otherwise, we'll need skips and trucks.'

'You're not putting cement anywhere near my truck,' said Frank, when he was asked.

'Have you got citric acid to stop cement setting in Frank's truck?' asked Rooster.

Jamie ran up the hill and phoned Simmo. 'Have we got citric acid?'

'Ah,' said Simmo, sounding as if he was rolling about in bed with yet another woman. 'I wasn't expecting a cement job so soon. Tell you what, just order some catering packs of sugar from a Cash & Carry. That'll stop cement setting. Put it on the company credit card.'

'You never gave me a company credit card.'

'Ah,' said Simmo. 'Get Rooster to pay.'

'I'm up a hill.'

'I thought you were breathing heavily,' said Simmo. 'To be honest, that's a bit of a relief. I thought you were getting pervy on me.'

Jamie rolled his eyes. Unfortunately he rolled them in the direction of Anouska's house. There, he saw a naked man stomping around, gesticulating wildly. Anouska had a shirt on and nothing else. She was giving everyone a right eyeful. And there, bang in the middle of it all, was Antonia. She was reclining on a chaise longue and was totally naked. All this appeared to be for the titillation of Benjamin and Vladimir who, for the moment at least, were totally clothed.

'Are you still there?' said Simmo.

'Not to worry,' said Jamie, 'just watching my ex-girlfriend participating in an orgy with a famous artist, an MP, a Russian gangster and some other bloke with a small cock. Remind me, what is the sugar for?'

'Sugar will stop cement from setting. Make sure the pH of any liquid you transport is no higher than 9.'

'There's just one problem,' said Jamie.

'What's that?'

'I haven't got any pH paper.'

'Ah,' said Simmo. 'I will be sending you a full lab kit. Honest. I'm sourcing it as we speak.'

It sounded like Simmo was getting his ears nibbled as they spoke.

'Buy twenty 50 kg sacks of sugar and throw them about like there's no tomorrow. Believe me, nothing will set.'

'I don't believe a word that comes out of your mouth!' Jamie yelled.

He was watching Anouska giving Antonia a drink of wine – from mouth to mouth.

'Keep your head and keep the receipts,' said Simmo woundedly. 'Now the next batch of water that comes might not be quite so fresh. It will be a little green in colour. Don't panic. Just make sure you add some biocide.'

'I haven't got any biocide!'

'I'm working on it as we speak.'

At this, Jamie tossed the phone into the grass. Simmo warbled on for a few more seconds. Then there was blissful silence. Jamie lay on the grass and looked at the clouds. He could see the planet Venus gleaming in the morning light. It was so far enough away that not even the oil industry could pollute it. It was a consoling thought.

*

Fletcher waved a truck through. It bore the logo of a cartoon "Snappy Dragon". It turned out that the only place Jamie had been able to source sugar from was a Chinese Cash & Carry.

'Think how much Sweet & Sour Sauce that lot could have made,' said Fletcher, as a couple of roustabouts unloaded the van.

Rooster patted Jamie on the back. 'Thought I'd seen it all, son. Then you go and organise a Chinese delivery for me.'

The cementer had shown up in a big red truck with a cement unit hidden in the back. Another truck, a bulk tanker full of cement powder, parked nearby. The cementer attached a few hoses here and there and was soon ready to go.

The roustabouts lined three skips with plastic, ready for the excess cement. Frank and three mates showed up with old tankers and they delivered some green water.

'What swamp did that come from?' said Rooster to Frank.

Frank shrugged.

'You got biocide?' said Rooster to Jamie.

Jamie shrugged.

'Alls I can say is: "Amen for Surrey money". They don't ask shit.' Rooster shrugged.

What happened next was incredible.

The cementer started the truck's diesel engine and began mixing cement. When he began pumping, water came back into the tanks. When the first tank was full, Frank sucked it all into his truck and drove away. This was repeated another two times. When watery cement came back, it was diverted into skips. Jamie threw sugar at it. Then pure cement came back and it was put into skips too. Jamie threw the remainder of the sugar at that. Just when the cementer stopped pumping, the last skip was filled. The cementer then washed up and flushed everything through to one of Jamie's tanks, from where it was sucked up into the last truck.

It was a textbook job. They had done their sums properly. Nothing had been spilled. It was, Jamie thought, a miracle.

After a few high-fives and a bit of a tidy-up, the boys headed for the brothel.

Alan headed home, chased by a one-legged man.

Chapter 28 - What Alan Made

The Vicar was on the steps of the pub. The Vicar was blind drunk. He'd watched the trucks coming and going with detached bemusement. With six pints of Upside Down inside him it was easy to regard everything with detached bemusement.

Having drilled a hole in the ground and removed the displaced earth in skips, they appeared to have stuck a big pipe in it and were now filling the hole with cement. Lots more trucks came and went. Skips came and went. Whores had arrived. It was all getting rather Biblical.

'This is Sodom and Gomorrah,' the Vicar said to no-one in particular, wafting an empty pint glass at the vista.

He wondered if humankind's biggest sin was simply to be too busy. There was a lot of palaver to create a hole through which toxic juices would flow back and forth. No good would come of any of it. Profits would be made. Whores would be fucked. Pollution would be created. An environment destroyed. Then they would all move on and do it again somewhere else.

The problem was that "somewhere else", for the moment, was Foxhole Down.

And this, the Vicar thought, got to the heart of the matter. The lottery that determined "somewhere else" was a fix. Someone had made sure that everything happened somewhere else. The entire point of places like Foxhole Down was that they never became somewhere else. That was why sleepy old vicars like the Vicar were put there to die.

The natural order of things had been upended. Someone had made a quite deliberate decision to visit evil upon the village. The world had indeed become smaller.

The Vicar was joined on the steps by Fletcher, who was sipping a pint of Upside Down.

'Fletcher!' said the Vicar delightedly. 'I take it you're no longer barred?' The Vicar loved forgiveness.

'I think the Major realised that if the drilling mob were turning the cricket pavilion into a whorehouse, they couldn't get too sniffy about me. Happens my money's now as good as the next man's.'

'And are you stealing a lot?' the Vicar enquired innocently.

'Coining it in, Vicar.'

'Jolly good,' said the Vicar. 'Everyone else is participating in the rape and pillage. I don't see why our local champion should be left out.'

'Jesus couldn't have put it better himself,' said Fletcher, lighting a roll-up cigarette. 'Talking of which, you'd better put in an appearance at the cricket pavilion. It's what he would have wanted.'

'Oh dear,' said the Vicar. 'I was hoping that no one would think of that. I'm not looking forward to it. I'm more used to dealing with white collar sinners.'

'And they're red knicker sinners,' Fletcher winked.

'There are so many sinners attached to this particular enterprise, I don't really know where to begin. Do you know who is behind all of this?'

'A bunch of bastards from Surrey by the sound of things,' said Fletcher. 'Land of Hope and Glory Drilling? Sounds like a joke to me. Someone's having a big laugh at our expense.'

It was at this point that Alan strode past. He was walking as fast as he possibly could - without breaking into a run. This made him look like a walking contestant in the Olympics, albeit a geriatric one. Limping after him, as fast he could go on one leg, was the one-legged derrickman.

'That don't look hopeful,' said Fletcher. 'Do you think we should intervene?'

'I'll drop by later,' said the Vicar. 'They need to talk.'

'About what?'

'About missing legs.'

*

The siege at Alan's lasted for less than five minutes. He got home. He bolted the door. He drew the front curtains closed. He locked himself in the toilet. He sat on the toilet. He buried his face in a towel. He held its soft folds tight against his ears.

A pesky, muffled knocking sound still made its way through. Why weren't towels thick and fluffy any more? He could hear that someone was shouting something. They were making a scene, Alan thought. Although digging up the village green and drilling an oil well on it had made a pretty big scene in itself.

'Blah blah blah blah blah,' said Alan like a child, trying to drown out unwanted words.

He thought about phoning the police. But then they would find out. Everyone would find out. It would be the end of him.

Alan lowered the towel.

'You can't hide,' said the Latino voice, cracking. 'I will find you in the end.' Then he said something ominous: 'Others will come.'

Alan desperately wanted to use the toilet he was on. He lowered the towel into the bath and went to his front door. He unbolted it. He opened it. There, in front of him, confronting him, was Carlos. There was no hatred in his eyes. Just determination.

'Come in and have a cup of tea. I'll put the kettle on. I need to use the bathroom. I won't be a minute. Please, have a seat. Make yourself comfortable,' said Alan.

When Alan returned, Carlos had indeed made himself comfortable. He had taken his leg off.

'A chicken has come home to roost,' said Carlos.

His leg was propped up against Alan's Victorian mahogany pedestal games table, the one with the Tiffany lamp on it.

'Colombian coffee?' said Alan.

Carlos scratched his stump and nodded. That would do.

As Alan prepared the coffee and biscuits, he weighed his options. His future in the village was in this man's hands. What did he want? Revenge? Money? An explanation?

Alan decided that he wanted to die here, in this house, overlooking that green – even if that green had an oil rig on it. This was his last stand. He would pay.

Alan broke out the nest of rosewood parquetry tables and served coffee and biscuits.

Carlos drank steadily. He was careless with the crumbs.

At length he spoke. 'I have been a long time on one leg,' he said. 'This day has been a long time in coming. Your house is not how I imagined it. I expected something much much bigger.'

'I live modestly,' Alan said.

Carlos smiled. 'I have thought about you for many years. I swore I would find you one day. You'll excuse me if I take a little time?'

Alan nodded. Oh my God, he thought, he's come to kill me.

Carlos's eyes drank in every detail of Alan's hobbit-hole. From the curtains to the carpets, the wall coverings and Alan's odd ornaments.

'There is no woman's touch in this house,' said Carlos. He looked at Alan. 'And there is no woman's touch about you.'

'I never found the right girl,' said Alan sadly.

'You don't even have the touch of a whore on you. You should get over to the cricket pavilion. While you still can.'

Thank the Lord, thought Alan. He hasn't come to kill me at all. Yet.

Carlos took a knife out, flicked it open and began picking his teeth.

That's really really not good, Alan thought. 'What do you want from me?' he asked.

'Hospitality.'

'My house is your house.'

'I paid for it with my leg.'

'Actually, it's a family house,' Alan began. He didn't finish.

'Did you inherit the business also?'

'No.'

'Ah, an entrepreneur. You spotted an opening in the market. For creating maimed and disabled humans.'

'Please..'

'I will please myself,' said Carlos. He was stern now. 'You are lucky I don't kill you, you son-of-a-bitch.'

Carlos dug his knife into the occasional table. Alan smiled weakly.

'I wouldn't blame you for cutting my throat. I deserve it.'

'You deserve a much slower death than that. You deserve to suffer for years.'

Alan didn't want to look at Carlos. He could feel his head going down. He resisted it. He didn't want it to appear as if he was hanging his head in shame. He still had his standards to maintain.

'How many Alan? How many? How many deaths? How many children? How many legs? Did you ever think of us?'

Alan shook his head.

'You are not an imaginative man, are you?'

Another little shake.

'You are the perfect man for your business.'

'What do you want from me?'

'Everything. Or nothing. Sometimes life is punishment enough. You will never forget me, will you?'

'No.'

'We should all come. You should have to meet every one of your victims. There must be thousands.'

'Possibly.' Alan had never dared to think of the possibilities.

'You had good years. You had less good years. Always there was product going out of the door. You didn't bother yourself about the customers. How did you find them? Did they find you?'

'There were arms fairs. The government were very good.'

'Your products are still out there. Silently waiting on another farmer. Another child.'

Carlos took the knife and ran the blade back and forth across his carotid artery.

Alan felt a fierce stab of panic. Were Carlos to kill himself, it would stain the house indelibly in Alan's mind. He wouldn't be able to go on living there.

There was a trickle of blood coming down Carlos's neck.

'You can have anything you want,' said Alan. 'I am a wealthy man.'

The knife kept moving.

'I am a wealthy man. I have a net worth of twenty million pounds. Thirty million dollars. Take it. All I want is this house and a modest pension.'

The blood kept flowing.

'Please stop!' Alan cried. 'You can have the house too. And my pension.'

'Alan!'

It was the Vicar.

Carlos removed the knife from his neck.

He pointed the knife at Alan.

'Padre, let me introduce you to Alan Somerfield. Former owner of Foxhole Industries. He is the man who made land mines. And he is going to hell.'

Chapter 29 - It All Gets a Bit Weird

Things accelerated. It was the usual fatal oilfield collision of rig, crew, chemicals and cash. They had access to too much money.

Once they started drilling, they couldn't stop themselves. There was something called a seventeen and a half inch section. It went on for about three days. Then something called thirteen and three eighths casing was run into that hole and cemented into place. Then there was something called a twelve and a quarter inch section. It went on for even longer, a week maybe. And they then ran something called nine and five eighths casing into that hole and cemented it too. They were repeating themselves - in increasingly smaller scale.

More skips came and went for the rock that they were removing. More green water arrived. More chemicals. More cement. There was more bobbing up and down by the whores in the Jacuzzi. There was lots of that.

There were more guards in the woods.

'There used to be bears in those woods,' said Fletcher, watching two chubby blokes tentatively spilling out onto the road before heading back for cover.

Jamie and Fletcher had struck up an odd friendship borne out of the number of trucks and tankers that came and went on Jamie's behalf. They had gotten into the habit of sharing their 9 am bacon roll together in Fletcher's security cabin with a cup of tea.

Simmo had finally delivered for Jamie in terms of chemicals. There was still no proper drilling fluids program for Jamie to follow. There was still no proper lab kit for Jamie to test the drilling fluid to check whether its properties matched those in the non-existent program.

Jamie was literally working in the dark. Carlos the derrickman had gotten into the habit of waking Jamie up in the early hours of the morning when the mud looked a bit stodgy. With his pyjamas under his overalls, Jamie would eyeball it, suggest that either water or Soda Ash or both were added, and head back to his bed.

He had no idea what Soda Ash was, or did. But it worked a treat.

'You'd love Simmo,' said Jamie.

'I doubt it,' said Fletcher. 'The man sounds like a total criminal.'

'Exactly,' said Jamie.

'Why on earth would I want to consort with that type?'

'Because you are that type?'

'I'm an honest thief,' said Fletcher indignantly. 'I rely on total integrity – from my victims. All the criminal classes do is lie to each other and shop each other to the police. How am I supposed to work with that?'

'I hadn't thought of it like that,' said Jamie. 'There's more to dishonesty than meets the eye.'

'Look at us,' said Fletcher. 'Where would I be if I couldn't rely on you?'

He was right. Jamie showed Fletcher all the chemicals that he had and then Fletcher helped himself to a few sacks of what he fancied would sell. Jamie charged it off as used on the well. Surrey money paid for everything. It worked a treat.

Fletcher split the proceeds 50-50 with Jamie. Of course Jamie knew that nothing of the sort was happening, Fletcher was Fletcher, after all. Jamie was grateful for the money, whatever percentage he was actually receiving. Antonia had cleared their accounts out completely. Jamie was building up a stash of cash. He would need it for when he finally went on the run. The well was proceeding too quickly for him. Every day's drilling brought his doom a day closer. For the moment, he stayed. If they'd found Scottie in Cornwall, he didn't have much hope for his own chances on the run. He lay in his grotty cabin every night, trying to figure out some kind of negotiating strategy with the Russians. Clearly, they weren't the "forgive and forget" types. Jamie wasn't sleeping well.

*

'Land of Hope and Glory Drilling, whoever they are!' Jamie and Fletcher clinked pint glasses in the pub after a cement job.

A man walked past carrying a couple of canvases wrapped in cloth. This delivery man had become a regular visitor in the past week. He knew where he was going. Upstairs.

'What is that evil lesbian Spanish cow up to?' said Jamie.

'Them's paintings,' said Fletcher.

'You want to see what that girl's installed up there,' said the Major.

Jamie and Fletcher lowered their glasses. They looked at each other and looked at the Major.

'She's got a temperature and humidity controller on the go. I'm charging her extra for the electricity,' said the Major.

'Of course you are,' said Fletcher. 'You're a bigger crook than I am.'

'She's put extra locks on the door and she won't let anyone in,' said the Major. 'I'm charging her extra for that too.'

'I can only dream of scams like yours,' said Fletcher. 'But where's the fun in making money legitimately?'

'You like a scrap, don't you Fletcher?' said the Major.

'I love it.' Fletcher grinned toothily.

Jamie looked long and hard at Fletcher. He'd had an idea. Perhaps the man whom everyone else shunned and feared was Jamie's best last hope. Perhaps his savior had been there in front of him all along.

'How do you fancy taking on some Russian gangsters?' said Jamie.

The light in Fletcher's eyes told Jamie all he needed to know. Fletcher wasn't the kind of man to take murder attempts in his own home lightly. It was an offense to his sense of propriety. It wasn't the kind of thing that he would take lying down. He had guns.

That night Jamie moved in with the Fletchers and slept like a baby.

*

The next morning, Jamie and Fletcher broke in to Antonia's room. Fletcher knew a back way up to the upper floors of the pub and he had the locks picked in no time. He was a trained locksmith. It was the best money he had ever spent and amounted to the sum total of his higher education.

They counted twenty paintings, stored in a specially-made rack which ensured that they didn't touch or damage one another.

Jamie slid one out. It was mainly green in colour. Trees and a few buildings. Not much sky.

'It's a bit fuzzy,' said Jamie.

'It's total shit,' said Fletcher.

'Do you think she's learning to paint?' Jamie asked. 'It doesn't look very Spanish.' He turned the painting around. 'The wood doesn't look very new.'

'I know how to date a painting,' said Fletcher. 'We'll check the houses for satellite dishes.'

The two men stared at the houses in the painting. Never mind satellite dishes, there wasn't even a hint of a TV aerial. Or a car. Or a road, even.

'I can't make out shit,' said Fletcher. 'Whoever did this had bad eyesight. I reckon it's one of them posh holiday resorts like Centre Parks where you have to leave the car at the gate and there's no telly.'

'The houses all look a bit ramshackle,' said Jamie.

'Yeah but they'll be luxury inside, with free bars and everything,' said Fletcher. 'The trouble is, the rich bird that painted it doesn't know her arse from her elbow and she's made a right cunt of it. Doesn't have the talent to paint roads or cars or satellite dishes.'

'I knew Antonia was nuts,' said Jamie. 'But this proves that she's totally unhinged. What the fuck is she doing with our money?'

The next painting was a small ship in a storm with about a dozen people on board.

'Now that's class,' said Fletcher. 'I'd have that in my front room. Although, he's been a bit heavy with the white paint on the left hand side.'

Clearly, to Fletcher's mind, good artists were men and bad ones women.

'That could be worth something,' said Jamie.

'It's not very big,' said Fletcher.

'What's size got to do with it?'

'Everything! The bigger it is, the longer it takes you to do it. The more you charge.' Fletcher looked at Jamie in disgust. 'You're obviously a fucking moron.'

'I think the name on it counts more than the size,' Jamie retorted.

'None of them have got names on them!' Fletcher shouted. 'I'll put this one over your head in a minute. See how much that makes it worth.'

They took all the paintings out and Jamie photographed them. There was a yellow one with "Café" written at the top. It was a real mess. All straight lines at weird angles and squiggles.

'Look,' said Fletcher. 'There's a boob in the middle. And a baby with his arm in the air. I can't believe that people get paid for that shit. I can't make out a café anywhere.'

There was a strange painting done on wood with a young man in a beret, chemise and furs, sitting by a window sometime in the past.

'Who the fuck paints on wood?' said Fletcher. 'And I'll tell you another thing: that guy in the painting's a poof.'

'No he's not, he's Italian,' said Jamie.

'Same thing.'

Fletcher was so disgusted with the art that he didn't want to steal any of it. This came as a blessed relief to Jamie, who suspected violent Russian involvement. And in his present state of emotional fragility, he wanted as little to do with Antonia as possible.

The art didn't bode well. It related to a world which was far beyond Jamie's ken. It was being used in a game of poker, whose stakes for Jamie couldn't have been higher.

Chapter 30 - Red Dawn

Jen's life had leapt boldly out of its previous dreary prison and had slipped itself between the pages of the most fabulous magazine. Her life was now part Country Life, part Harper's & Queen's and, thrillingly, a whole lot of Cosmopolitan.

For years she had stared at those models in those magazines, with their fabulous faces, their fabulous bodies, their fabulous clothes and their amazing boyfriends. It had all seemed so close but it had also seemed to be ridiculously unattainable too. She now realised that wealth in itself wasn't enough. You needed to have attitude too.

With that devil-may-care / footloose and fancy-free / I-can-take-anything-life-throws-at-me attitude, Jen had blossomed into the woman that she should always have been in the first place.

There was nothing that could stop her now.

And what a life she was having. Lying here in her bed, still feeling the warmth of him, she felt as if she was in a dream. They were having lunches in sleepy country pubs. They were having super-indulgent shopping trips in town. They spent long wistful hours together staring out of the window, watching the roughnecks bickering on the drillfloor. Life was perfect.

Things had turned out unexpectedly on the man front. On two fronts. Obviously a woman like Jen would never normally have considered taking up with an oil rig worker, so Hamish was a turn-up for the books. The other turn-up for the books was the man that she had discovered beneath the shaggy Scottie-dog exterior. He was the most amazing, attentive, lyrical lover. When they went out together in London, Hamish turned into what could only be described as a dandy. As a couple, they turned heads. Away from the rig and the village, he was a totally different man. He knew all the smartest and most sophisticated places to go. She had to admit that he was doing something to her that she would never have imagined. He was teaching her things.

She was so blissfully in love. She could hear her man rattling about in the kitchen downstairs. He was probably making her a cup of tea – another unexpected delight. Soon he would be back in her bed, back in her arms, whispering loving things and kissing her in unexpected places.

Then something unexpected happened.

Jen heard the front door close. Then silence. She moved over to the window. Yes, Hamish was walking away. Ominously, he was carrying a holdall. He would never normally leave without coming in to kiss her goodbye. If he was leaving, it was usually just to nip over to check that everything was all right on the site. Jen literally saw red.

There was a note on the kitchen table.

Jen wondered how prominently notes on kitchen tables featured in those perfect magazine lifestyles. She opened it.

My darling Jen, My work here is over. It is time for me to move on. Our moments together have been precious and extraordinary. Your touch will linger in my heart forever. It has been an amazing sixteen days and twelve hours. When we first met, I was looking for the village slapper. Well I certainly found her. The sex was substantial, sustaining and spectacular. You slapped me good and proper. You slapped my head. You slapped my heart. You slapped my soul. You slapped me in such a way that I will never be the same again. Yet I must go. Our love cannot be. You deserve better, my angel. I am a false man with a false heart. I destroy things – that's why I'm in the oil industry – and I would have destroyed you too. I have made a whore of you, but you will never be like the others. The poetry of your motions was as good as any Shakespearean sonnet. I am a stammering Limerick by comparison. I love you too much to become the weight around your neck. I will always be your most ardent admirer. I will always be your social inferior. Forever, Hamish x

PS Suggest you look for a Zak Goldsmith, upper-class, top totty, environmental-type. H x

Tears flooded down Jennifer's convulsing cheeks. In an instant, her magazine life had slid from the lifestyle spread and careered headlong into the agony pages. If she wasn't careful she'd be looking up one of the counselling services in the small ads at the back. She was now and would forever be a woman abandoned by note. There was some cheer in that. It was better than being dumped electronically. She at least had something she could burn. Or keep forever.

Yet he was right. She was too good for him. Deep in her heart she had known that it was a doomed romance. When they came to write the novel of her tragic affair, it would be called "Forever Hamish". They could get Kate Winslett to play her and Ewan

McGregor to play him. Or maybe Gerard Butler and the dragon queen from Game of Thrones. Yes, that was better. It made her feel better. Briefly.

No, Jennifer's heart was definitely broken and she howled anew. She had fallen in love with the worst man in the world – a lying, whoring, Scottish oil rig worker – and her life was over. It was as simple as that.

Through her tears, she looked out of her front window at the ecological disaster unfolding on the cricket pitch. This time she really was looking through a red mist.

There was something wrong.

Jennifer stifled her sobs. She moved tentatively to the window and dried her eyes. No, they weren't playing tricks on her. The windows of her cottage were actually red.

Jennifer went outside. There was a strange smell in the air, which was industrial and vaguely toxic. Queerer still, her side of the village green had been turned a pinkish red colour.

Others were coming out of their cottages, wandering like lost souls, struggling to come to grips with what exactly had happened.

They didn't have to wait long. Rooster had gotten hold of a bullhorn.

'Okay, listen up, residents of the east side of Foxhole Down. We've had a gas leak, but it's nothing to worry about. It has taken on a red colour from the rocks we just drilled through. This will wash off your houses in due course. Anyone seeking compensation can pick up a claim form from the pub. I have been assured that Surrey money will take care of everything. However, anyone caught reporting this to the media, Tweeting it, or Facebooking it will not receive any compensation and will be sued for defamation. Surrey money has deep pockets. Stay on their right side. Don't say you weren't warned.'

With no heart for a fight, Jennifer turned around and shuffled back inside. The other residents did exactly the same thing. They were all defeated. Their enemy was too great. They would take the money while they could. The truth was, the houses looked rather jolly in pink. They were listed. They would be restored. Eventually. Surrey money had very deep pockets indeed. Everything that was unfolding in the village now had a terrible inevitability to it. What was the point in resisting?

Jennifer brought her duvet downstairs, so that she could snuggle up on the sofa. What she needed was two weeks lounging in her pyjamas, drinking buckets of tea, eating huge slabs of chocolate and watching eighteen hours a day of crap drama.

*

The first explosion of the morning blew away the trailer holding Jamie's chemicals. The Vicar, praying fervently in his church, was knocked off his kneeler. Alan, ordering spares for the whorehouse Jacuzzi, fell off his chair. Jamie, trying to spy on the shenanigans in the Rectory, fell out of his tree and knocked himself unconscious.

The device had been planted in amongst the pallets of chalk. A large puff of white dust shot across the drill site on one side and over two cottages on the other. The roof of the trailer was blown clean off and a large virgin-white mushroom cloud rose two hundred feet in the air.

Jennifer, watching from the fastness of her sofa, thought it rather pretty and was quite moved. It seemed like an omen of better things to come.

The Vicar, emerging unsteadily from his church, saw God Himself rising right in front of him. This was enough to send him straight to the pub.

Jamie awoke to find Anouska loosening his clothing.

A broad smile broke across his face. 'Okay honey,' he sighed. 'Let's get to it. You did it with her. You can do it with me. Not quite sure if I can perform, but I'll have a go. Let's do all that sensual arty stuff for about six hours.'

'Don't be ridiculous,' Anouska growled. 'I'm performing first aid. You're concussed.'

Jamie looked around and saw that he'd been laid out on a chaise-longue in Anouska's studio. He could see the upside-down heads of an English gangster and a Russian MP.

Anouska placed a cool wet face-towel on Jamie's forehead. It felt wonderful.

'Shag me now Anouska. Then let the boys kill me. I'll die happy.'

'There will be no killing in this rectory,' said Anouska. 'It's a place of creation.'

'Jamie?' Vladimir tapped his face. 'What do you know about the paintings in Antonia's room?'

Jamie wondered why he should tell them anything. Then he remembered why he should tell them everything.

Before he knew it, he was propped up in front of a computer screen. It was like being shown mug shots of criminals, only in this case the pictures were of paintings. Jamie must have been shown two hundred, but he was able to pick out several of the canvases he had seen.

'What do you think she's up to?' Anouska said to Vladimir, once the viewing was over.

'You're asking me?' Vladimir replied. 'You're the art expert.'

'You're the criminal expert,' Anouska retorted.

'How did she get them?' Vladimir wondered.

'Remember, they've been on the run for quite some time,' said Anouska.

'Don't look at me,' said Jamie. 'I've been dumped.'

'She's had full access to my computer,' said Anouska. 'All my contacts. Some of dealers are definitely dodgy.'

'Would she be able to work out which dealers they were?' Vladimir asked.

'Given that they were in a folder marked "Dodgy", I should think so,' Anouska replied ruefully.

Vladimir shook his head.

'I'm an artist! These are dealers I wouldn't touch with a bargepole. I've got nothing to hide on my computer. My scams, as you keep reminding me, are entirely legitimate.'

'Are these paintings worth anything?' Jamie asked.

'You know the one of the holiday homes with no satellite dishes?' said Anouska.

'Yes.'

'They've got no satellite dishes because it was painted a hundred years ago. Heard of a guy named Cézanne?'

'Sounds like a magician,' said Jamie.

'He was a magician,' said Anouska. 'That canvas could be worth ten million quid. And you know the one of the boat in the storm? The one you said you'd have in your front room? That's by a guy called Rembrandt.'

'I've heard of him,' said Jamie, pleased with himself.

'Fifteen million quid for that one. And the one on the panel?'

'The guy who looked like a.... Looked a bit gay?' said Jamie, rediscovering his political correctness.

'Yes, that poof is a guy called Raphael. If you go to Rome, you'll find his body buried in a building called the Parthenon.'

'That one will be worth a couple of bob then.'

'That poof's self-portrait could be priceless. Does the name Picasso ring any bells?'

'Who hasn't heard of Picasso?' Jamie laughed.

'He did the café where you can't see a café. With a boob in the middle and a baby's arm.' Anouska arched an eyebrow.

'Art's not really my strong point,' Jamie confessed.

'Stick to holes in the ground, darling.' Anouska patted Jamie lightly and patronisingly on the head. She whispered in his ear. 'The Picasso. Twenty million.'

'Just how much money did Antonia have at her disposal?' Vladimir asked.

'She took everything I had left,' Jamie wailed. 'Three million quid.'

Vladimir nodded. Sums were adding up. 'Looks like she has spent wisely.'

'These paintings,' Jamie said. 'I take it that they're all stolen?'

'Which is exactly where I come in,' said Vladimir. 'I have all manner of crooked friends who would do anything to possess one of these paintings. I could make a killing.'

Vladimir grinned at Jamie.

'The Raphael wasn't stolen from an art gallery,' said Anouska. 'It was looted by the Nazis.'

Vladimir's eyes lit up. 'That would make it worth even more to a Russian,' he said.

'Jamie darling,' said Anouska, 'please don't ever call Raphael a "poof" again.'

'Sorry,' said Jamie. 'I was repeating what Fletcher said. He seemed to know more about art than I did.'

'"Poof" isn't a term we use in art,' said Anouska tartly. She turned to Vladimir. 'The sooner he's dead, the better.'

'Why would I want to kill him?' said Vladimir. 'When I can use him as a bargaining chip?'

Jamie looked up. Something had just reared its magnificent and noble head. A thing called hope.

Chapter 31 - WTF ??

Jennifer didn't need copious amounts of opiate drugs to numb her pain. She had television.

And here she was, up in the highlands with a "Roaming in the

Gloaming" romance. It was all kilts and curls and kisses. There was the heroic, passionate highlander. There was a bonnie lass with a heart to be won. There was the obligatory evil landlord with hints of dastardly Englishness about him. And he had dastardly sheep too. It was right up Jennifer's present alley. And she didn't even know where "the gloaming" was. But these were the kind of Scots you could rely on.

It had got to the bit, fifteen minutes in, where the couple were about to make hay in a hayloft when a headstrong young cousin bursts in to warn of the imminent arrival of the dreaded redcoats.

The line was delivered by the kind of actor who only gets two or three lines in the entire movie. The line was delivered by the kind of actor who either goes on to great things, or whose career sinks without trace.

The line was delivered by…. Hamish.

'Lachie! Morag! Run!' said Hamish.

'What the fuck?' said Jennifer.

She paused the movie and took a closer look at the callow face on her screen. Yes, it was definitely him. Fifteen years younger, but unmistakably Hamish.

And then it all started coming back: the soap opera appearances; the small roles in episodes of detective dramas; the token Scotsman in costume dramas; the minor feature articles in magazines. She had seen him before. He wasn't a part-time dandy away from the rig. He was a full-time dandy dressing down in Foxhole Down. Why? He was making good money. She knew that. She'd read it. He did pantomime, for goodness sake.

Perhaps fracking in Foxhole Down was the biggest pantomime of all.

'What the fuck?' said Jennifer.

*

In the blind panic after the morning's first explosion, there was only one place for the stunned inhabitants of Foxhole Down and the startled drillcrew on the village green and the horrified whores of the cricket pavilion to congregate. They all went to the village pub. Why, even some of the zombified incomers showed up.

The Vicar and Inspector Witcher were in a corner of the snug. Both were drunk.

'You're a disgrace to the cloth,' said Witcher.

'You're a disgrace to the force,' said the Vicar.

'No I'm not. I'm off-duty. I'm here as a sightseer.'

'There are no sights here.'

'This is the sight to end all sights.'

'What sight?'

'The sight of the end of the world as we know it.'

The Vicar nodded and drank.

'Are you going to come quietly Vicar? Or am I going to have to call the heavy squad?' Witcher leaned in and whispered, 'I know that you planted the bomb.'

*

There was a knock at Jennifer's door. It was Grassy Knoll.

'I love you,' said Grassy. 'I've always loved you. It took this mayhem to make me see the truth.'

'Grassy!' Jennifer yelled. 'Stop right there!'

'You're the love of my life!'

'No I'm not! I'm the woman you're going to make a fool of yourself with.'

'I'll love you until the end of time!'

'I find you fat, repellent and socially inept. Let me save you some time.'

Grassy wilted.

'Oh Grassy, please don't start crying. I'm simply trying to save you from the same mistake that I just made. I've chosen completely and utterly the wrong man. He's the wrong class, the wrong background, the wrong financial strata, the wrong personality, the wrong hairstyle, the wrong moustache. Good grief, he's from the wrong country! How wrong can a girl get?'

'I don't care about what's right and what's wrong, I only know that I love you,' said Grassy, desperately trying to rally.

'How many women have you met recently?' asked Jennifer.

'Well, there's you and Anouska. I'm terrified of Anouska.'

Jennifer stroked Grassy's hair. 'Sweetheart, you need to get out more. Come in.'

Jennifer, strangely energised by this unexpected declaration of love, strode around the room, wearing her duvet like a cape. She looked out of her red window.

'This entire village needs to get out more,' she mused. 'Look what's happened to us. We've allowed ourselves to be taken over by incomers who had no feel, nor love for the village itself. We buried our heads in the sand as village life died. We pretended that the outside world could be kept at arm's length. Now we have the worst incomers of all. And they have fucked us royally.'

'At least I was a conspiracy theorist,' Grassy mused.

'And I'm sure that there's a wonderful conspiracy theorist out there for you,' said Jennifer.

'But I'll need to get thin, attractive and socially confident first,' said Grassy bitterly.

Jennifer grimaced.

'What happened to your ideal man?' said Grassy.

'Turns out he was a lying, scheming, preening love rat, who wasn't even an oilman at all. He's a small-time, low-budget, bit-part player in historical romances, TV mini-series and UK soap operas, with occasional forays into pantomime.'

'What the fuck?' said Grassy Knoll.

*

The second explosion of the morning blew Alan's cottage to pieces.

The device had been expertly placed. The central supporting wall was completely demolished. Glass blew out both ends of the house, peppering the back garden and shooting across the road at the front. The house folded in on itself haphazardly, the roof sagging in the middle.

Carlos the derrickman wasn't seen again in the village.

Alan found himself in a place beyond tears. It was the worst thing that could have happened to him.

'I wish I'd been inside,' he said. 'We could have gone together.'

Rooster was ever the pragmatist. 'Look on the bright side,' he said. 'The exterior walls are intact. The rest can be rebuilt. It'll be as good as new.'

'I preferred it old,' said Alan. 'To die in.'

'Don't be selfish,' Rooster chided. 'The Good Lord will make his decisions for you. Death isn't a lifestyle option.'

*

The bombing campaign was, like so many village issues before, sorted out in the snug bar of the Royal Oak.

'The Vicar is up to his neck in doo-doo,' Inspector Witcher began.

'I'll happily die in prison with the poor and the oppressed,' said the Vicar. 'The way the global economy is going, it's the only place I'll be guaranteed a dry bed and three square meals a day.'

'Spare us the martyr act Padre,' said Witcher. 'Now who provided the explosives?'

'I did,' said Alan, glumly.

'And where did you get them?' Rooster asked.

'They're from my business.' Alan gathered himself. 'I used to make land mines.'

There was a gasp. From Antonia.

'What the fuck?'

'Nowt wrong with landmines, mate,' said the Major. 'Saved my bacon often enough.'

'That would be the bacon you were cooking in Aldershot, sergeant,' said Witcher. 'You were never a major and you've never seen action. You could be what's called a minor major.'

Antonia gasped again.

'What the fuck?'

'Makes sense,' said Alan. 'Not officer material. I always suspected you were a wrong 'un.'

'I wasn't the one blowing peoples' legs off,' said the Major.

'You've deceived us all this time,' said Jennifer.

'Doesn't take much in your case, given how quickly your knickers hit the floor when that Jock con man twitched his moustache,' said the Major.

Grassy Knoll lunged across the bar at the Major.

'And you were so busy with your conspiracy theories, you couldn't see what was under your nose, you idiot!' the Major added.

Rooster pulled Grassy back.

'Okay, everyone just calm down!' Anouska shouted.

'That's easy for you to say,' said Jamie. 'You've caused more havoc than anyone.'

'Shut up!' said Antonia.

'People! People!' shouted Vladimir.

He was brandishing a revolver. This succeeded in gaining everyone's attention.

'Inspector Witcher, please continue,' said Vladimir.

'Who blew Alan's house up?' said Witcher.

'That would be Carlos the derrickman,' said Fletcher.

'You knew?' said Alan.

'I thought he was burgling you,' said Fletcher. 'I wasn't going to snitch on him for that.'

'You really are the lowest of the low,' said Alan.

'No, I think that turns out to be you,' said Fletcher.

'Leave him alone,' shouted Grassy Knoll.

''Don't you get on your high horse,' said Anouska. 'I've seen your investments. There isn't a scumbag company on planet earth that you wouldn't take a punt on.'

Vladimir laughed raucously and did a little more brandishing.

'You are all on your high horses. And you are all scum. Look at you. I'm the only honest crook here.'

Vladimir motioned with his gun for Inspector Witcher to continue.

'So we've had two explosions,' said the Inspector. 'We can either: throw the Vicar into the slammer and hunt Carlos down like a dog; or we can say fair's fair, let the two incidents cancel one another out, and not trouble the authorities.'

There were murmurs of approval.

'How do we explain the damage?' said Grassy Knoll.

'We'll blame it on British Gas,' said Witcher.

'There is no gas in Foxhole Down,' said Jennifer.

'Believe me, my colleagues aren't bright enough to notice,' said Witcher.

'So everything is settled?' said Antonia incredulously. 'And after all this shit, you all act like nothing happened?'

'That, my dear, is the secret of our success,' said Anouska. 'Welcome to England.'

'There is just one side issue,' said Vladimir. 'I believe that you have started a little art collection?'

Antonia looked calmly at Vladimir. 'Yes? Some minor pieces. I hope to make a nice profit on them. I didn't like having my money in the bank. Too vulnerable. And the art market is hot.'

'And from what I gather, these paintings are pretty hot too. I would consider taking them off your hands.' Vladimir's smile was that of a vulture's.

'I'm sure we could negotiate a price,' said Antonia nervously.

Vladimir stroked his chin with his revolver. 'Why should I pay anything? After the losses I have suffered?'

'Hear hear,' said Jamie.

'But we agreed..' Antonia's voice tailed off.

'Why do people have such trouble understanding dishonesty?' said Vladimir.

The Vicar shrugged.

Vladimir hit his stride. 'I enjoy lying. I enjoy stabbing you in the back. I love making you cry.'

Tears were, indeed, making an appearance in Antonia's eyes. 'They represent everything we have!'

'Even better!' said Vladimir.

The tears ran down Antonia's cheeks. 'Why can't you just kill my ex-boyfriend? Then everyone is happy.'

'It's not dishonest enough,' said Vladimir.

'What could be more dishonest that murder?' said Antonia.

'Murder and theft combined?' said Vladimir.

Then a remarkable thing happened. There was a discussion. More pints of Upside Down were drunk. Inspector Witcher gave a legal perspective. The Vicar weighed in with some spiritual and moral advice. An agreement was reached.

Vladimir would take the paintings from Antonia. He would have them verified in secret by Jasper. If they were found to be genuine originals, then they would be accepted as payment for the lost cocaine. Jamie and Antonia would be free to go their separate ways. If the paintings were forgeries, then all bets would be off and Jamie would have to run for his life. Antonia, whatever the outcome, would be spared. Jamie struggled to follow this part of the argument, but it involved references to the Madonna, the Eastern Christian church and Russian superstition. In short: it was bad luck to blow Antonia away, but Jamie was fair game. The bombs had been dealt with, the red houses would be restored, Alan's would be rebuilt and Carlos would be allowed to run free. The Vicar even agreed to hand over his remaining stash of high explosives. Strangely enough, almost no one had any problems with the continuation of the brothel. It was felt that the village had bigger fish to fry. In the meantime, drilling was to recommence.

Everything had been sorted out down the pub over a few ales. There had been no dramas. There had been no arrests and no need for fisticuffs. Vladimir even presented Witcher with his revolver, which turned out to be an ornament – and a valuable one at that. There was a warmth and an optimism in the air. Everyone agreed that it was just like the good old days.

Jamie walked away from the Royal Oak in a light-headed mood. He was saved.

'What the fuck?'

Chapter 32 – Jesus Saves

It was with a heavy heart that the Vicar approached the brothel.

It would have been a dereliction of his duty not to go. But with every reluctant step, the word "duty" bore down on him, reminding him of that other duty that he had regularly performed in marriage. This was of course, the same duty that these professional girls were forced to perform. Maybe they had a little in common after all.

'Padre, we have been expecting you.'

There was an over-dressed, overly made-up middle-aged woman standing in front of him, smiling. She was not overtly pretty, but was unmistakeably intelligent – and this made her very attractive.

To his horror, she took him by the arm and led him towards a room. God alone knew what was going to happen in there. The Vicar himself couldn't begin to contemplate. He was terrified.

They sat at a table.

One of the girls came in.

She was carrying a tray.

The Vicar, aghast, stared at its contents.

There were two cups, two saucers, two spoons. Milk and sugar.

They were going to have tea.

On her way out, the girl took a poster down. It had diagrams on it. It must have been a price list.

So they were in a perfectly pleasant room in a perfectly pleasant cricket pavilion. The Vicar noticed that his companion was wearing a perfectly pleasant floral-patterned dress. Presently, some perfectly pleasant tea arrived. And cakes.

'My name is Chrisanna, in case you were wondering.'

'I'm Simon.'

'I'll call you Padre. That works better.'

The Vicar was relieved. Being called Padre somehow made sex acts with multiple prostitutes less likely. What he feared most was these girls' generosity.

'Have you come to save us, Padre?'

Simon the Padre cleared his throat in an attempt to find his tongue. 'You have become part of my parish. It's a professional courtesy. I gave a blessing to the rig.'

'You have come to bless us?'

'I don't think that would be appropriate.'

'But what we do here is far less damaging than what the rig does?'

Chrisanna smiled perfectly pleasantly. She cocked an eyebrow and tilted her head.

The Vicar was being dragged into a moral debate that he had neither the stomach nor the wits for.

The Vicar forced on a smile. 'Only the Good Lord could give a definitive answer to that.'

'But surely you have an opinion?'

In all his years ministering to the wealthy, the Vicar could barely remember being asked to venture much of an opinion on anything at all. Except the stock market. Simon could see that the Brothel Madam's smile was more beatific than he could ever manage. He was a fraud. And he knew it. What was worse, she knew it too.

'I'm not going to beat around the bush,' he said. 'I disapprove of everything that is going on in this cricket pavilion. Or on this green, for that matter. I have grave reservations about our economy, particularly the oil industry. I will give you a blessing if you want one. But I will be blessing your souls and not your activities.'

'You never said that to the drill crew. Is it because we are women and you think you can push us around?'

Simon thought about this deeply. 'I suppose it is,' he said. Even as he said them, the words shocked him. Did his entire moral

philosophy boil down a simple fear of strength? It appeared that it
did. It also appeared that it could be changed pretty quickly too.

Chrisanna laughed. 'Finally. Honesty.'

Simon smiled. He could feel a burden lifting.

'I will spare you my homilies, if you will spare me yours,'
Chrisanna said.

'You have worked out a moral landscape for yourself that you
are comfortable in?' Simon asked.

'Of course.'

'And you are spiritually at ease with your maker?'

'God? Yes.'

'Then I am happy to know you Chrisanna. And happy for you.'

'But you still disapprove.'

'I am in no position to cast any stones.' The Vicar giggled. He
felt like a Christian. A real Christian.

'I was going to offer you a joint,' said Chrisanna, 'but I think
you are giddy enough, Padre.'

'Yes,' the Vicar giggled.

'Do you mind?'

'Who am I to judge?' he tittered.

Chrisanna lit up. The Vicar sat back, enjoying the aroma,
beaming.

'I DO have a beatific smile,' Simon smiled.

Chrisanna didn't understand.

'Beatific. A smile full of holy bliss.'

Chrisanna smiled one of her own.

'You see?' said Simon. 'Your one is better than my one.'

'I have nothing holy,' she laughed.

'But you do! You're a natural. You emanate spirituality. You could do my job better than I could.'

'Not better. Different. I could be a preacher, it is true. But no homilies.'

'I can't imagine why I was so frightened to come here,' said Simon.

'I think that you knew you would have to confront something. Perhaps something deep within you. There are no businesses like this in the villages where you preach. Your flock is careful to export its sins. May I ask you a personal question?'

Simon nodded.

'Did you love your wife?'

'How did you know I was married?'

'Do you not think that I can recognise a married man? Do you not think that I know my business? And you haven't answered my question.'

'We had a functional marriage.'

'So you have had sex. But you haven't loved.'

Simon nodded.

'And you came here with your disapproval?'

Simon brightened. 'Yes, but that was the old me. From ten minutes ago.'

Chrisanna took a deep draw and smiled. 'I guess I threw a little stone there myself Padre. I apologise.'

'See? Nobody's perfect. I guess that's what Jesus was telling us all along.'

'You spend five seconds forming a judgement and you lose the plot completely.' Chrisanna laughed.

'I lost the plot for forty years.'

The two of them hooted with laughter.

They shared another pot of tea and spoke frankly about their lives. Chrisanna was about to retire. The Surrey Money had pushed her over the top financially. Like many in her business, she had been running away from her past. Strangely, she had found herself and had flourished rather than being destroyed. She saw it for what it was: a lucrative business with some dangerous downsides. But money bought muscle and trouble was easily dealt with. She had kept moving and was about to settle down finally – far away from her past.

Simon knew that he was going to die right here. He had some ministering to do first.

When he left, it was Simon who took Chrisanna's arm. They strolled together, under the shade of the trees, to the roar of the rig's engines.

'You have changed my life,' Simon said.

'And it didn't cost you a penny,' said Chrisanna. 'I must be going soft. It is time for me to retire. I am turning into a tart with a heart.'

'What's wrong with that?'

'They get their throats cut.'

Chrisanna's laugh was devilish. Simon found himself liking her even more for it.

They spoke no more. The Vicar had everything and nothing to say. She had done everything and nothing for him.

She had saved his soul.

Chapter 33 - Life's a Gas

Having drilled out the shoe on the 9 5/8 inch casing (don't ask), they were on the last section of drilling. This meant that they were headed to encounter oil or gas, or maybe both, or maybe neither. It was an exciting time.

It was particularly exciting for Jamie. His new derrickman, Carlos's replacement, was useless. On the bright side, at least the water they were using was no longer green. There were other issues with the water.

'Great news on the water front,' said Simmo, when they had last spoken.

At this, Jamie's heart sank.

'We've got a new supplier,' said Simmo eagerly.

It was the eagerness in Simmo's voice that made Jamie's heart sink even further. He knew instinctively that Simmo wasn't paying for this water. He was being paid to take it away. God alone knew what toxins it contained. Jamie wondered whether any nuclear reprocessing plants were offering special deals. He wouldn't have put it past Simmo to import radioactive water from the Fukoshima disaster in Japan. Anything could go down the well. There was no oversight from the government whatsoever. The groundwater 300 ft under the North Sea was better protected.

Jamie wondered whether the whole fracking scam was simply a way for the corporations to get rid of their toxic waste. The global elite would live far from these disaster zones. Jamie had thought that the global elite lived in places like Foxhole Down. The villagers of Foxhole Down had thought they were the global elite. They were wrong.

Simmo was definitely far away. Jamie heard seagulls in the background – and they didn't have British accents. 'Where are you Simmo?' he said.

'Just outside Antibes,' said Simmo.

'Are they fracking there?' said Jamie.

'Hell no. I think France banned it.'

Jamie was moving to France.

The drilling was going well. Jamie could tell. They were filling skips with rock cuttings like nobody's business. Jamie couldn't tell if they had struck oil, or whether the gas detectors had picked anything up. He would have had to ask the loggers. He would have had to ask Antonia. He couldn't even bear to look at her. He had taken to wandering the woods at night, being chased back into the village by the security guards. He was miserable. He was heartbroken.

Things took a fateful turn when Rooster called everyone together for a meeting. Jamie arrived last and then took up a position on the same side as Antonia, but three people along. He could pretend that she wasn't there.

The big news was that they were about to frack.

Rooster outlined the state of play and the way forward. Due to some incredibly clever technology, they were now drilling horizontally through clay. This clay, it was suspected, held the precious gas that they sought. The bad news was that there had been very few shows of gas so far. This was indicative of one of two things: either there had been no signs of gas because this was the type of rock that needed to be fracked to release said gas; or there was no gas and the well was a "duster".

Jamie had no idea why gas would ever want to show itself, but even he knew that a "duster" wasn't a good thing. Imagine spending all that Surrey Money to get a load of dust?

It was fracking or bust.

The rig pumps weren't deemed strong enough to perform the fracking, so a special high-pressure pump truck was coming. Now the fracking fluid was deemed so toxic that everyone involved in the job was to wear special nuclear, chemical and biological hazmat suits. Rooster brought out a sample and one of the crew put it on. It looked like something from a dystopian science-fiction movie.

They were to perform the fracking looking like lime-green cybermen.

Rooster then caused a stir by announcing that the whorehouse in the cricket pavilion would close during fracking procedures. The crew were less than happy about this.

'You pick the most stressful time of our operation to close down our biggest source of stress relief?' said a cut-throat roughneck.

There was then some to-and-fro about whether the girls could continue operations wearing the hazmat suits. There were obvious difficulties associated with this. Rooster was adamant that anyone on-site caught not wearing a suit would be run off. It was finally agreed to provide the girls with suits and see what happened. It was getting to the end of the well. Rooster had a bank account stuffed with cash. He had little to lose.

'I normally have to test any fluids that go down the well,' said Jamie. 'Do you want me to test the fracking fluid?'

'Are you insane?' said Rooster. 'Do you want to die? What the hell are you going to test it for? To see if it's poisonous enough? This is the worst liquid in the history of liquids!'

'Could I at least have a Geiger counter?' Jamie pleaded.

'The fracking fluid ain't radioactive,' said Rooster.

'It's the water Simmo sent that I'm worried about,' said Jamie.

*

Foxhole Down at sunrise on the fracking morning was a surreal sight.

A light mist caressed the village green. The red light of dawn nicely set off the blushing cottages contaminated by the gas leak. Lime green cybermen went methodically about their business, connecting metal pipework to a large orange truck. Three lime green cyberwomen bobbed quietly in the outdoor Jacuzzi of the brothel, awaiting the first business of the day. Alan came out of his temporary home with a bowl of porridge. He ate it on the steps of the church. He was joined by the Vicar, his new landlord. They were both tucked up nicely together in separate cots in the vestry. Alan was coming to terms with his past. The Vicar had been very forgiving and had stopped drinking. The two men had, quite naturally, fallen in love.

'Shouldn't you be dressed up as a spaceman too?' said the Vicar.

'I only coordinate the equipment,' replied Alan. 'My job is to stand back and watch the catastrophe unfold.'

Given Alan's previous work, this was an unfortunate choice of words. There was a brief, awkward silence.

'I'm sure it will be fine,' said the Vicar soothingly. 'What could possibly go wrong?'

There was a long, awkward silence.

'Given the high pressures and the toxicity of the liquid being used, why haven't the villagers been given protective suits?' enquired the Vicar politely.

'Because it's all perfectly safe,' lied Alan politely.

'I wonder what the bishop will make of this,' the Vicar wondered.

'Of what?'

'Of everything.'

Everything now included cameras. Anouska had mounted several remotely-controlled camcorders in trees and on buildings around the site. A producer in the rectory was controlling the entire operation.

A drone hovered overhead. Whether it belonged to Anouska, MI-5 or the CIA seemed a moot point.

Things kicked-off when the diesel engines in the pump truck started up. They roared. A plume of smoke was sent skywards.

Jennifer, hypnotised, watched it from the front steps of her house as it drifted slowly across the village.

'Looks like something from the industrial revolution,' said Hamish. He was standing beside her.

For the second time in her life, Jennifer gracefully described a perfect parabola with her hand and belted Hamish across the cheek.

For the second time in his life, Hamish's eyes watered as a result.

He rubbed his Caledonian jaw. 'I guess I had that coming.'

'Oh you've got a lot more coming to you than that.' Jennifer buried her face in Hamish's, her lips reaching eagerly for his. She pulled him inside the cottage.

As they tore each other's clothes off, Hamish confessed to everything: the lies, the sexual exploitation, the minor roles in soap operas. He'd taken the Surrey Money. He set out to break her heart, but had ended up breaking his own. He was a bankrupt. He wasn't worthy of her. He had nothing to offer her but his heart. And other tired old clichés.

It no longer mattered that he was wrong. He was hers. Forever.

There was grunting. There was revving. There was lots more smoke. There was sweating and pressure testing. As Jennifer and Hamish lost themselves in each other's bodies, the truck went into overdrive and fractured Mother Earth herself. Toxins were pumped deep into her fissures.

Meanwhile, Jennifer realised that she was dicing with pregnancy. She didn't care. She was in a heaven beyond anything she had ever known. What on earth did they teach these boys in the Highlands? Hamish was not only hitting the spot, he really was making the earth move. It intensified her pleasure tenfold. This man was a Love God.

But the earth was actually moving.

'Don't stop,' Jennifer wailed.

'I canny give you no more,' said Hamish, rolling onto his side and falling out of the bed.

'Hamish! Come back! Don't leave me again!'

'I'm not going anywhere!' Hamish shrieked. 'I can't get up! It's an earthquake!'

Jennifer reached out with her arm and pulled Hamish back into her bed. The tremor subsided. They surveyed the damage: a few skew-whiff pictures on the wall; Jennifer's teddy on the floor; the photograph of Jennifer's mum and dad's tasteless 80's wedding face-down on the dressing table.

'They shouldn't have been watching us in the first place,' said Hamish. 'It was freaking me out.'

'Good,' said Jennifer. She pecked him on the cheek.

And so they made their recuperation in each other's sweaty arms, mixing feelings of bliss and anxiety.

'I wonder if there will be any after-shocks?' said Hamish.

'I don't know,' said Jennifer. 'I'm just worried that it might hit me in Tesco's. That would be embarrassing.'

'I'm not talking about orgasms,' said Hamish. 'I'm talking about more earthquakes.'

The entire village could have shaken itself into rubble as far as Jennifer was concerned. She was in love. They would run away, far from the noise and the smoke and the fracking pollution. They would find a little cottage in the Tuscan hills where no one would bother them and they'd grow a few olives and raise a few children. Life would be simple and beautiful and loving. Just like it used to be in Foxhole Down.

Jennifer sat up.

'This is shit,' she said.

'I know,' said Hamish. 'They've gone too far this time.'

But things had only just started to go wrong.

*

The earthquake played merry havoc with the drinkers in the Royal Oak. Most of these were actually rig workers still in their lime green hazmat suits, whose main concern was drinking the beer before the vibrations caused them to spill it. Fixtures and fittings flew off the wall. Alan and the Vicar fell into each other's arms. Anouska and Antonia rolled about on the floor together, giggling their heads off. Benjamin and Vladimir jiggled on their barstools, looking on jealously. Jasper the art dealer surfed it out on his own, looking rather splendid and elegant. Fletcher and Grassy Knoll sat it out on a bench, looking entirely non-plussed.

When the shaking was done, the recriminations began.

'I'm glad you think it's so funny,' Grassy shouted at Anouska.

'Oh come on,' said Anouska. 'Things are so bad, you've got to see the funny side.'

'This is the end of everything!' Grassy yelled.

'Just because Jennifer wouldn't shag you, there's no need to take it out on us. The only thing that will sort you out is a quick innings in the cricket pavilion.'

'You sexist cow!' said Grassy. He turned to the drillcrew. 'I suppose you all know about my humiliation?'

The drillcrew nodded.

'You should be grateful you've still got a village to gossip about you,' said Fletcher.

'Not for much longer at the rate things are going,' said Alan.

'Why, has someone laid landmines in the woods?' said Antonia.

'Shut up, you thieving Spanish slut!' said the Vicar.

'You shut up, you failed …. shepherd. What kind of a Vicar has no flock? You're supposed to save souls, not abandon them,' said Vladimir.

'He has saved a soul. Mine!' said Alan.

'"Mine?" That's an unfortunate choice of words,' said Benjamin Latham MP.

'Hark at the biggest scumbag in the village,' said Fletcher. 'You've brought ruination to this place. You look down on me and you've caused more damage than fifteen generations of Fletchers.'

'Stop tearing each other to pieces!' shouted the Major. 'Come over here at once! Everyone!'

The Major could be commanding when he wanted to be. Everyone dutifully trooped over to the bar.

'Watch this.'

The Major turned on his water tap. It spluttered. He lit a match and held it under the tap. A huge flame shot out. The tap was like a Bunsen burner.

'That's our water supply,' the Major said.

'We're fucked,' said Grassy Knoll.

Chapter 34 - This is Serious

'This is serious,' said Rooster.

It was indeed so serious that some of the incomers had showed up at the pub. They were so bewildered that they hadn't even ordered a drink. They just stood there.

'It looks like we've got a bad cement job on the nine and five-eighths casing string,' Rooster went on. 'And the gas that's been released by the fracking is migrating up past the casing and into the water table. We might have to perform a squeeze job.'

'I don't care if you give the well a blow job,' said Alan, 'just stop the toxic gas.'

Rooster replied sharply. 'The gas isn't toxic. It's perfectly natural.'

'It's not natural coming out me fucking tap,' said Alan.

'You haven't got a tap,' said Fletcher. 'A one-legged man blew your house up in revenge for your evil landmines. You've looked down on me your whole life and you're no better than an MP.'

Fletcher looked around at the villagers. 'You're all scum!' he said.

'If the gas is natural, does that mean I can bottle it and use it?' asked the incomer.

'You can bottle it, label it, and stick it up your arse,' said Grassy Knoll. 'Does everything have to be about personal gain? Who the fuck are you anyway? If you're going to come to this pub, you'll buy a fucking drink. It's an ancient tradition.'

'I don't drink,' said the incomer.

'Then fuck off,' said Grassy Knoll.

'I've lived here ten years,' said the incomer.

'Then you should have fucked off ten years ago.'

Grassy shook his head. He shrugged his shoulders. He fell silent.

'Anyhow!' Rooster cried. 'The good news is that the Surrey Money is going to compensate every household by ten thousand pounds.'

'Twenty thousand,' said Fletcher.

'Ten thousand,' corrected Rooster.

'That makes all the difference,' said the incomer. 'So long as it's quickly tidied up.'

The incomer went out.

Grassy Knoll let out a long groan. 'Please give me another pint, Major. I like to imbibe toxins on my terms. Let me enjoy my beer before these bastards poison it.'

'Rooster?' said Anouska. 'I'll see you in hell for this.'

*

Before she saw anyone in hell, Anouska had to see something else: Antonia's paintings.

'This is serious,' said Anouska. She was looking at a painting with a magnifying glass.

They were all gathered in Anouska's studio – Antonia, Vladimir, Benjamin and Jasper the art dealer.

'This, my dear friends, is, in my humble opinion, a Rembrandt.'

She was looking at the striking canvas of the boat in the storm-tossed sea.

'Why would you know?' said Vladimir. 'You are just an artist, not an art expert.'

'The benefit of being "just" an artist is that they let you in to the National Gallery at night. And you can spend as much time as you want looking at the masterpieces. Undisturbed. With a magnifying glass. And I'm telling you that's a Rembrandt.'

Vladimir looked at Jasper, who was agitated.

'They're all originals!' Jasper squealed. 'I've found a treasure trove of missing masterpieces! Picasso! Cézanne! Rembrandt! Raphael! Raph-fucking-ael! I'm in a place beyond orgasm. Kill me now, my life will never surpass this moment.'

'That can be organised more easily than you would like to imagine,' said Vladimir gravely. 'Tell me, how can you be sure that these are originals?'

'I can't wait to tell you,' said Jasper gravely. 'The brushwork, as Anouska alluded to, is a perfect match. This is the easiest part to fake. However, I've had these canvasses x-rayed and there are areas that have been painted over – as an artist would do with a work-in-progress. That is very very difficult to fake. I have also checked the frames, the wood and the canvas, where appropriate. This is impossible to fake. And these are perfect matches for the originals.'

'And you would stake your life on that?' said Vladimir.

Jasper nodded solemnly.

'I'll take them,' said Vladimir.

'And what do I get?' said Antonia.

'Your life.'

'And what about Jamie?'

'He will be killed in due course. Tomorrow.'

'No!' Antonia shouted.

Vladimir smiled. 'Aw, it must be true love.'

'You have no right to all these works.'

'You bought them with money you stole from me.'

'We stole nothing from you. We stole from John Webster after he was dead. The cocaine was added by Jamie to his drilling fluid by mistake. We owe you sixty million dollars. Nothing more.'

Vladimir laughed. 'Sixty million. Plus interest.'

'Then take all of the canvasses.'

'I'll take them all – if they're originals.'

Antonia moved closer to Vladimir, almost squaring up to him.

'As originals, these are worth more than two hundred million dollars. But I can offer you a far more beguiling proposition.'

Slowly, a smile appeared on Vladimir's face.

'Go on,' he said.

'These paintings are all fakes.'

'What the fuck??!!' Jasper spluttered. 'You ignorant Iberian idiot! What do you know?' He turned to Vladimir. 'I'd stake my reputation on the fact that these are originals.'

Antonia turned to Vladimir. 'I met the forger.'

Vladimir's interest was piqued. 'Why should it be more beguiling to me that these are forgeries?' he asked.

Antonia smirked. 'Because it will enable you to swindle some of your biggest rivals – and some of your best friends. They will have these paintings of their walls and in their private galleries, and only you will know that they are forgeries. Think how much pleasure that will give you.'

The temperature in the room appeared to drop by several degrees as Vladimir gave Antonia his iciest stare. Her life, Jamie's life, hung in the balance.

Then Vladimir threw his head back and laughed.

'You dirty Spanish bitch! You know me so well! What fun is there in selling legitimately stolen paintings to a bunch of crooks? How much better to sell illegitimate forgeries of legitimately stolen paintings to a bunch of crooks? It's perfect! They'll be falling over themselves to outbid one another for these. Paintings that they can never openly exhibit! That'll teach them to be crooked!'

Vladimir strode over to Antonia and held her shoulders Russian-style. 'You are the most amazing, scheming bitch I have ever met.'

Antonia nodded modestly. 'I have even provided a respected art expert to vouch for them.'

'I resent being used like this,' said Jasper.

'You'll resent an early grave even more,' Vladimir replied

'So Jamie and me are free to go?'

'Of course!' Vladimir cried. 'I'll cancel Jamie's assassin.'

They toasted the venture with champagne. In all the excitement, Vladimir forgot to make the call. When he remembered, all he could get was the killer's answerphone message. He was in a place that had no mobile signal. He was in Foxhole Down.

It was, indeed, serious.

Chapter 35 - Laughing Gas

Footage of the burning taps spread rapidly across social media. The reaction veered, disappointingly, more towards PMSL and LOL than OMG or WTF. Foxhole Down was frequently characterised as being rich and somehow getting its just desserts, or that its chickens were going home to roost, or even that, in the grand scheme of things, the village's problems didn't amount to very much.

It appeared that pollution fatigue had set in on planet earth.

As in so much else, America had got there first. The cavalry had hardly come galloping to the rescue of the hundreds of thousands of citizens suffering from the deleterious effects of fracking there. The Russians had drained the Aral Sea and nobody had noticed. The Chinese were choking their own people to death and the rest of the world glibly bought their plastic toys with nary a squeak of protest.

What hope was there for a prosperous, picturesque little village in Hampshire?

'We'd have got more support if we were a plotline in Downton Abbey,' said the Vicar, glumly.

'Downton Abbey don't exist and more people believe in that than believe in us,' said Fletcher. 'Just goes to prove that when people stop believing in God, they don't believe nothing. They believe everything.'

Fletcher was rewarded for this by being offered a cigarette by Anouska. She lit it too – with a wink – and lit her own. She then lit Inspector Witcher's cigar. At this, half the drillcrew lit up.

They were all in the pub. The joint was jumping. It was the Major's best night ever. Flushed out by the gas, more incomers had shown up. They were about to complain about the smokers.

'Don't even think about it,' said the Major. 'You're going home tonight stinking of tobacco.'

'Tell your wives you encountered some wild people from the woods,' said Anouska.

She inhaled her cigarette. Then she exhaled it in the incomers' direction. And then she inhaled some laughing gas.

Anouska giggled and offered the facemask to the company. 'Have a laugh on me,' she said, 'while laughter is still legal.'

Alan had never expected that he would ever dabble in drugs. And he would never have dreamed that his first experiment would be with laughing gas. But he realised that in this topsy-turvy world everything was up for grabs. And he realised that if a man of his background and temperament was thinking that, then the world was more topsy-turvy than he could ever have imagined.

Alan inhaled. He tried to stop himself laughing, but couldn't. 'I've fallen in love in my seventies!' he laughed. 'In a hand-holding kind of way. My house was blown up and I don't care!'

The Vicar took a deep breath. 'I was put here to guide a few old souls to their deaths before I died myself,' he tittered. 'But this old soul has found his soul mate. And that's rather wonderful.'

The Vicar kept a hold of the gas and took another lungful. 'I thought it was the parish that was dying, but it turns out it was the village.'

The Vicar laughed raucously. And so did everyone else.

The Major grabbed the gas. 'I have been a fraud from the minute I moved in here,' he giggled. 'But who in Foxhole Down wanted a Non-Commissioned Officer when you could have a Major?'

The regulars let up a cheer. The incomers stood, looking perplexed.

'I've learned a lot in the past few weeks,' laughed the Major. 'Mainly that I'm the least fraudulent person in the entire place. The MP's a fraud. The Government's a fraud. The media's a fraud. The Vicar's a fraud. Our resident artist is a self-confessed fraud. Our reliable old village elder is a right old fraud. Our virginal spinster is a fucking fraud. Our resident thief is a dependable fraud. The drillcrew's a fraud. Land of Hope and Glory Drilling is an offshore tax fraud. But I ask you to salute the biggest fraudsters of all.'

There was a gasp of anticipation.

'The incomers! Who posed as villagers! Who didn't take any part in village life at all! Who hadn't a fucking clue what living in a village meant! What could be more fraudulent than that?'

The incomers stood and took it.

The Major took a couple of deep breaths of gas and continued. 'Go back to your wide screen televisions! Go back to your internet! Go back to your rancid supermarket wine! You have no personalities. You are everything that I despise about modern life! You have ruined my business! Fuck off the lot of you!'

The incomers fucked off.

Everything that the Major said had been greeted by a cheer – apart from the incomers. The incomers departed to a rousing cheer from everyone.

Grassy Knoll took some gas. He paused. He chuckled. Then he let rip. 'I told you so!' he shouted. Then he sat down, a contented conspiracy theorist.

Fletcher took a measured breath. 'You can put as much poison down there as you like. You'll never drive the Fletchers out of Foxhole Down. We're like cockroaches!'

This received a thunderous round of applause.

Jennifer sashayed into the pub, looking sultry, sassy, and sexually satisfied. She was trailing Hamish behind her. She took a breath.

'Love is everything,' she breathed 'You can frack the village. But he,' she waved a finger at Hamish, 'has fracked my heart.'

'Awww,' said everyone.

Hamish had a couple of gulps. 'We're madly in love. The village is madly in madness. But fear ye not, humble villagers. This will all blow over once the changed climate has blown us over.'

Rooster grabbed the facemask before Hamish could do any further damage. He took the biggest breath of anyone. He was a big man. He had a big laugh.

'There's nothing to worry about folks,' he smiled. 'There is no gas. The well is a duster. No money for the Surrey money. The village is safe!'

There was a huge cheer.

Rooster took another heroic suck. 'There may be some toxins circulated out, but Jamie will capture them. Everything will be cemented up. The well will be plugged and abandoned!'

There was mayhem. People were cheering, hugging and high-fiving. Anouska ordered champagne for everyone. Jennifer and Hamish kissed passionately. Alan and the Vicar held hands.

Antonia came in. She went straight to the front to address everyone. She didn't take any gas. She looked very worried.

'Has anyone seen Jamie?' she said.

Chapter 36 - Plug and Abandon

It wasn't just the well that was to be plugged and abandoned. Jamie was to be plugged and abandoned too.

He emerged from the ancient wood at dawn, looking the worse for wear, soil on his face and twigs in his hair.

'I made a run for it,' he told a sleepy-eyed Major over breakfast in the Royal Oak. 'One of the security guards jumped me. Wrestled me to the ground. Told me I wasn't going anywhere. They tie-wrapped my hands and stuck me under a tree for the night. Kicked me back into the village half an hour ago.'

'Antonia was looking for you,' said the Major.

'I couldn't give a flying toss if I never saw that Iberian idiot ever again,' said Jamie.

Alerted by the sound of his voice coming up through the floor, the Iberian idiot duly came down. She took Jamie's bewildered head in her hands and kissed him tenderly.

'If you think that's going to make up for everything you've done, you've got another thing coming,' Jamie croaked.

Antonia pulled a twig out of his hair. 'Everything that I did, I did to save your life. The Russians are paid off. No one is coming to kill you.'

Antonia didn't know this, but she was speaking a very dangerous untruth. After failing to make contact with the hit man, Vladimir had completely forgotten about it. Jamie's life had slipped his mind.

Looking deep into Antonia's eyes, searching for some vital truth, Jamie saw lust, betrayal and lesbianism. Lust won. Jamie let Antonia take him upstairs, where they made amazing, giving, sharing love.

They shagged each other senseless.

*

Jamie presented himself for the cement job in a dishevelled but blissful state. Rooster was glad to see him and immediately got Jamie to calculate exactly how much fluid would be coming back. The cement was going to fill the entire hole. Then they were pumping an excess of 25%. This was in case the hole was bigger than they thought. Or something like that. Jamie could barely remember. Although he thought that plugging and abandoning meant setting a number of plugs one on top of each other, rather than cementing the whole thing at once. Or something like that. He could barely remember.

Back up the hill, Jamie was multi-tasking, hiding from the guards and making a final call. 'Don't worry, it's all in hand. We'll send Frank with as many trucks as you need,' said Simmo, who sounded like he was sipping a cocktail on a Hawaiian beach whilst having a sex act performed on him by a local prostitute. 'This is the last roll of the dice with the Surrey money. Let's cash in.'

'Simmo, I'd just like to say something before I sign off,' said Jamie.

'Go ahead, mate,' said Simmo kindly.

'I think that you are a reprehensible human being. You're a symptom of everything that's gone wrong with this world and the reason we'll likely destroy it,' said Jamie earnestly.

'After everything I've done for you?' said Simmo woundedly.

'You left me in utter shit,' said Jamie. 'You would leave this village in utter shit,' he added. 'You are an utter shit,' he concluded.

There was a crack. A branch above Jamie's head fell on him. Across the clearing, Jamie could see a small puff of smoke. He concluded that the security guards had started playing with air rifles, so he disappeared into the trees.

Back on the village green, everyone was wearing their hazmat suits in anticipation of some toxic fracking fluid coming back. It sent Jamie into a state of high nervousness. The soothing balm of Antonia's lovemaking was wearing off. The blind panic of not knowing what he was doing was setting in.

Jamie went back into Rooster's office to seek mathematical reassurance.

Rooster was looking relaxed – as relaxed as anyone could look in a hazmat suit. He was leaning back in his chair, the top half of the suit around his waist, his boots on the desk.

'Strangest goddamn cement job I've ever seen,' Rooster began. 'They want us to cement the drillpipe in place. That's what I call abandonment.'

'I'm worried about the volumes,' said Jamie. 'We can't put cement into trucks. We need to use the skips. They've taken half my mud pits away.'

'Strange that,' said Rooster. 'LOHAG insisted on it. Obviously don't want to risk cementing up the valves. Did you get those Chinese fellers to drop off another pallet of sugar?'

Jamie nodded. 'We'll take the drilling fluid back to the pits we have left. We take the fracking fluid into Frank's trucks with the rest of the drilling fluid.'

'What are they doing with the used fracking fluid?' said Rooster.

'I'm frightened to ask,' said Jamie. 'Simmo's cut a deal. I think the drillwater is radioactive.'

'Stand back and don't wave any Geiger counters around,' counselled Rooster.

Rooster was experienced in the ways of man's exploitation of the earth. He knew the score. He was very safe and very rich. Jamie liked him.

'We'll be done here soon enough,' Rooster continued. 'And they can keep the whorehouse or go back to cricket.'

'The whores are getting ready to leave,' said Jamie.

'Says it all,' said Rooster sadly. 'Things are pretty desperate when your whores walk out on you. So it's cricket for Foxhole Down - if they can muster enough men. Or watching grass grow. It's more or less the same thing.'

'I'm just worried about all this cement coming back,' said Jamie finally.

'For the last time, don't worry. The drillbit was wandering all over the place. The hole will be well over-sized. You won't get that much back. Now there's one question that I have for you: To fill the skips with cement, do you want a 4 inch hose or a 2 inch hose?'

'What's the difference?' said Jamie.

'Four inch is heavier, not so manoeuvrable. Two inch easier to handle, faster jet.'

'I'll go for a 2 inch hose,' said Jamie emphatically.

Who among us knows hoses? Unless it's the common or garden variety, most of us are clueless. Jamie certainly was. It is an arcane world of nozzles and pressures and velocities. Even with a casual acquaintance of the elegant equation brought to the world by Monsieur Bernoulli, one would require some experience of hosing cement to be so unequivocal. To be so certain and so ignorant was to be bullshitting.

Jamie didn't know it, but he had made a very fateful decision.

*

At the Toolbox Talk, Jamie wasn't able to follow events too well. Despite his reprieve, he had a sensation that things were not quite what they should have been. But they were drilling on a picturesque village green in Hampshire with a cricket pavilion converted into a whorehouse, so it was pretty bloody obvious that things weren't what they should have been. It was topsy-turvy world. Even so, Jamie had a distinct feeling that things had gotten worse.

The cementer was deranged too. He kept interrupting Rooster with daft questions about things that Jamie thought he should have known about. He seemed confused about whether he should be adding accelerator or retarder to his cement. Jamie suspected that this was rather vital.

There was another problem. The cement truck was parked on the other side of the derrick to where Jamie was positioned with his polythene-lined skips for the excess cement. It didn't make for great communication.

The deranged cementer was also hell-bent on pumping his 25% excess come what may.

'I'll get arrested if I don't,' he whined. 'It's those feminist lesbian tree huggers.'

That sounded to Jamie like the perfect description of Anouska. And, for that matter, Antonia. He was in love with, and had been betrayed by, a feminist lesbian tree-hugger. For a kid from a small town on the west coast of Scotland, this was quite an achievement. A disastrous cement job was small beer by comparison.

As Jamie looked around the room, he noticed that it was only Frank the tanker driver who had personalised his hazmat suit to make himself identifiable. Everyone else looked identical.

*

The cement truck's diesel engines gunned into life. Jamie wondered whether he would ever hear them again. He had decided that this was going to be the last cement job of his life.

The diesel smoke drifted across the sunlit roofs of the quaint cottages on the green and up towards the picturesque 18th century rectory with its leaded windows. The ancient woodland on the undulating down formed the perfect backdrop.

It was your typical idyllic village green cementing scene. Everything was being caught on camera by Anouska and her crew.

When the cementer began pumping, the first fluid that came back was Jamie's own, probably radioactive, drilling fluid. He was glad of the hazmat suit. One of the tankers was hooked up to the pits and began sucking at once. It was a reassuring sight and the truck made a reassuring sound. The poison which had afflicted the village, Jamie felt, was being drawn off. Four trucks came, four trucks went. Frank was the last to leave. He shook Jamie's hand warmly and waved cheerily as he drove off.

A colour change in the fluid returning denoted that the fracking fluid was now coming back.

Carlos's replacement, however, was an idiot. He might have held on to two legs, but he only had half a brain. Jamie's shout to divert back to the toxic sludge tanks fell on deaf ears, or to be more accurate, fell into a swimming pool of stupidity. Handles got pulled, fluid got redirected. All in the wrong direction.

Jamie felt sick to his stomach. He now knew that not only was this to be the last cement job of his entire life, it was also going to be the worst. He followed the path of the fluid in his mind and came to an awful conclusion, shortly before the liquid did.

'Oh shit,' he whispered.

The toxic sludge spewed out over the wire mesh fence and into people's front gardens. The derrickman panicked. He opened and closed any valve he could get his hand on. That made a big difference. Things got even worse. The spray got more powerful and gave the cottage windows a good dousing.

The toxic sludge looked really sludgey. And all too toxic.

By the time Jamie had got himself into a position to pull the right lever, the fracking fluid stopped coming back. It was more of his drilling fluid. So he diverted it back to the pits.

But the pits were full.

Jamie stopped to think what to do. His mind was swimming in the same pool of stupidity that belonged to the derrickman. It was a vast pool that all of humanity had dived into at one time or another.

Fluid was now overflowing the pits and oozing down the sides like a lemon meringue pie that outgrown its cake tin. To add to the effect, the pits had developed a foamy head.

Jamie finally managed to direct the fluid to the toxic sludge tanks. He prayed that there was no more toxic sludge to return. Although, judging by the state of the cottages, a second spray job would barely make much difference. Having gone through so much emotional turmoil in the recent past, Jamie found himself in a wonderful state: he didn't give a shit.

One thing was certain: Jamie's career in the oil industry was ending in ignominy.

The next thing due to return was the cement. The skips were lined up in front of the church, closely bunched to allow them to be easily filled by hose. Jamie gestured for the derrickman to position himself by the hose in readiness.

The derrickman glared back at Jamie. Even through the hazmat visor, Jamie could see that it was a really mean, horrible and nasty glare. Jamie felt really wounded. What was it with people? He was only asking a man to do what he was being very well paid for. The clown was responsible for the toxic sludge spill and hadn't even received a ticking-off, let alone been shouted at.

Sometimes, Jamie thought, the Conservatives were absolutely right about the workers.

Reluctantly, the derrickman sloped off to the skips. His body language could not have been more negative. It took the biscuit, it really did. However, the derrickman stood ready, with the hose in his hands, in a combative pose.

All Jamie had to do was divert the cement at the right time. They really really didn't want cement going into the wrong places.

There was a magic fluid that turned pink in the presence of cement. Jamie had forgotten to bring it. He stared hypnotically at the fluid rushing past him. He tried to calculate how many barrels were in 25% of 650 barrels. He tried to calculate how many barrels a skip could take if each skip was 160 cubic feet and there were 5.6 cubic feet in a barrel. He then wondered if six skips was enough.

Planning was everything. And Jamie hadn't planned.

The toxic sludge tanks made the decision for Jamie. They were full. Jamie diverted the flow to the hose, which he saw kick in the derrickman's hands. A nice, reassuring jet was spraying into the first skip. Shortly, the colour of the spray turned grey. It was cement. Jamie walked across the site and joined the derrickman.

This corner of the green was quiet. The din from the cement truck was reduced to a low hum. The loudest thing that Jamie could hear was his own breathing. They weren't even within shot of Anouska's cameras.

Even in a hazmat suit, the figure of Rooster was unmistakable. He appeared round the back of the drilling package. He was wearing a large set of ear defenders. His position during a cement job would be in the midst of the racket, on the cement truck, making sure that all was in order.

Rooster gave Jamie a thumbs-up.

Jamie gave Rooster a thumbs-up in return. This turned out to be a fateful gesture.

Rooster disappeared back to the cement truck.

At this, the derrickman motioned to Jamie to take the hose. The transfer was made gingerly. There was a fair bit of pressure on the hose. Jamie realised that the wider hose may have been heavier, but it would also have been more manageable.

Jamie presumed that the derrickman was going to the toilet. He reckoned that he would be all right, so long as they didn't increase the pump rate on the cement. Then he would really struggle to control the hose. He was only just hanging on as it was. Jamie held the hose firmly and watched the cement filling up the polythene-lined skip.

He then became aware that something was seriously wrong.

The hairs stood up on the back of his neck.

His throat ran dry.

He became gripped by fear.

Jamie turned his head. The derrickman had gone nowhere. He had, instead, picked up a large piece of pipe and was advancing towards Jamie.

This wasn't a derrickman. It was a hit man.

Jamie felt the blood draining from his head. He couldn't move. And no one was coming.

He was to be bludgeoned to death.

Jamie awaited the inevitable. His life did not flash by in front of his eyes, but he realised that there would be no escape from Foxhole Down. It was all going to end here. Antonia had lied to him. She had lulled him into the false sense of security that the murderer required. The sex had been fabulous. But she was a cow who had made a fool of him. They would have no happy ending. There would be no hacienda. In Andalucia. With satellite telly. There would be no children. There would be no grandchildren. Antonia was going to run away with everything. She was going to have someone else's babies – if she didn't run away with Anouska. Maybe they would adopt. Jamie, meanwhile, was to die alone and with no heirs. His DNA had reached the end of the road. He wondered if it was true that men ejaculated on the point of death. He certainly didn't have an erection.

Jamie felt himself move heavenward. He was leaving his own body. No, his body was coming with him. Faintly, in the background, he heard the din of the cement truck rising slightly in pitch. They were increasing the pump rate. His thumbs-up to Rooster had given the Louisianan the all-clear to let rip.

The hit man moved quickly.

The hose moved even quicker.

It whipped Jamie up into the air as the pipe smashed into the side of the skip and ricocheted off.

Cement was spraying everywhere: over Jamie; over the hit man; over the skips; over the cricket pavilion/whorehouse; over the trees; over the road; and all over the front of the church.

The hose whipped viciously through the air. It had abandoned Jamie and had left him beside his nemesis, who was retrieving his bludgeon.

Jamie froze again, stood in the grey rain. He could feel himself becoming heavier under the weight of the cement, even as his life ebbed away.

It wasn't his body he couldn't move. It was his mind. He would wait for his fate.

The hit man struggled to his feet, propping himself up with the murder weapon.

He turned. And sized Jamie up.

The two men were being hit with wave after wave of cement as the hose lashed back and forth.

The hit man raised his arm to deliver the coup-de-grace.

Jamie took his final breath. And waited for his end.

He heard a whistle.

He felt a breeze.

The hose whipped past Jamie's ear…

… and took the hit man's head clean off.

*

It took a while for anyone to realise that the cement was not going in the right place. They were all on the other side of the derrick, pumping blithely away.

Jamie woke up. He was being smothered in cement. He couldn't get up. He felt the pressure on his chest. He was going to drown, killed by an idiot cementer. It was more embarrassing than being betrayed by Antonia.

But here she was, coming to rescue him. Coming to kick him viciously in the side. After three or four hefty boots, Jamie broke free of the cement. Together, they scrambled clear of the cement rain and threw themselves under the drilling package and into each other's arms.

Jamie and Antonia kissed one another tenderly. Or, to be more precise, they head-butted each other through their hazmat visors. Jamie's ribs ached from the kicking Antonia had given them.

It was love.

Jamie's heart soared. Antonia's heart soared. The cement hose soared, dousing the church's 17th century stonework with 21st century gloop. The saints in the stain glass windows were obliterated. The cricket pavilion whorehouse wasn't spared either. Its gaily-painted wooden structure was quickly petrified, as were the adjacent cottages, the adjacent trees and the adjacent grass.

The hose whipped viciously back and forth, like a dragon breathing grey, stony fire. No one who saw it would ever forget it.

'It's biblical,' said Alan.

'It's apocalyptic,' said the Vicar.

They were standing on the steps of the Royal Oak, clutching a couple of pints of Upside Down. Neither thought to raise the alarm. They were both transfixed.

'It's out of control,' said Alan wistfully, 'but you don't want it to stop.'

'I never thought that the end of the world would be beautiful,' said the Vicar.

God was indeed working in mysterious ways. And it was all being captured in high-definition digital format by five artfully-placed cameras.

Anouska, standing outside her 1.5 million pound rectory in her three thousand pound trench-coat and twelve hundred pound boots, looked down on the scene and drew deeply and smugly on her Gauloise. Sometimes life was better than drugs.

The din from the cement truck lowered in pitch. The hose danced less violently. The flow decreased. It poured steadily into Fletcher's badly-tended front garden and then down the road and back onto the green. The truck's engines slowed still further. In a final theatrical flourish, the hose bowed its head and lay down.

On the cement truck, the cementer turned to Rooster and gave him a thumbs-up.

'The job's a good 'un.'

Chapter 37 - Cleanup

'Don't touch anything, this is a crime scene!' shouted Inspector Witcher.

'Don't touch anything this is a crime scene!' shouted Anouska.

Both had arrived at the Green from opposite sides, but had come to the same conclusion, albeit from opposite perspectives.

'Somewhere under there is a headless body,' said Witcher.

'Somewhere under there is a beautiful village green,' said Anouska.

'It came clean off,' said Jamie, 'bounced three times and then rolled off under the cricket pavilion.'

He was holding court in the pub to anyone who would listen, which was the Major, who had no choice.

Everyone else was outside, staring in awe at the incredible scene created by the combination of an oil rig, a village green and a flying hose.

It was a cement wonderland.

'It is magical,' said Antonia. 'It somehow makes the trees appear even more beautiful and fragile.'

'My cricket pavilion looks as if it has been melted,' said Alan.

'My church looks like it's been attacked by Satan himself,' said the Vicar. 'But it survived.'

'It's inspirational,' said Hamish.

'If that's the worst that Land of Hope and Glory Drilling can throw at us, then hooray for Foxhole Down!' said Jennifer.

'This mess is going to cost someone a fortune,' said Fletcher.

On this, he was completely and utterly wrong.

'It's ruined my front garden,' Fletcher wailed. 'And my prize-winning flowers.'

'Prize winning weeds,' said Grassy Knoll cynically.

Fletcher had made a half-hearted attempt to turn the cement in his front garden into a parking bay. He had been defeated by the weeds he hadn't cleared and by time itself. The cement had set too quickly for him.

Grassy Knoll continued. 'If THIS doesn't prove that there's a conspiracy against us, nothing will.'

'Conspiracy of idiots,' said Rooster. 'In hell's name, why did no one come and tell us to stop pumping?'

'Most of your crew were in the pub,' said Jamie, emerging from the pub. 'And I was fighting for my life with a hit man. With no help from the local constabulary,' he added, pointedly.

'We have been monitoring the situation very closely,' said Witcher. 'We didn't think he'd have a go during the cementing. Sorry.'

'So I've been used as bait?' said Jamie.

'Kind of,' said Witcher. 'I mean you don't think that I've been hanging around here because of a couple of minor explosions? There's a much bigger picture, you know.'

'Of course there is,' said Jamie, draining his pint. 'I'm just small potatoes.'

'No offence, but you are. If that guy is who we think it is, he's wanted in about twenty different countries. This is a major feather in our cap. The Americans will be delighted. I'll get a promotion.'

'What about my emotional scarring?' Jamie shouted.

'Oh shut up,' said Antonia.

'What is going on here?' Jamie yelled.

Everyone looked at the desecrated church, with its blanked-out saints. They looked at the petrified trees and the melted cricket pavilion / whorehouse. They looked at the cement-sprayed cottages on one side of the green. They looked at the toxic sludge sprayed cottages on the other. They looked at Witcher.

'We've been following Mr Rokossovsky and the Right Honourable Mr Latham MP for some time. There's been jiggery-pokery going on. Laundering drug money. Obviously we can't arrest them. Or I'd end up at the bottom of the Solent with a pair of cement wellingtons.'

'This is everything I've been talking about for years,' said Grassy Knoll.

'Oh shut up,' said Jamie, who didn't want to be usurped as the principal victim.

'But this works out perfectly,' Witcher continued. 'The books on about fifty murders have been closed. We've taken a major scalp. Our Russian comrade has to go home with his tail between his legs. Our corrupt MP goes back to cleaning his duck pond. Organised crime learns not to mess with the Hampshire Constabulary. And I get a big fat pay rise.'

This satisfied no one.

Grassy Knoll spoke for them all. 'Are you telling me that we've gone through all this just for a bit of money laundering? Is that it?'

'Sadly yes,' said Witcher. 'There is only one question that remains unanswered: Who is the criminal mastermind behind Land of Hope and Glory Drilling?'

*

To say that it was an unusual crime scene would be somewhat of an underestimate. The headless hit man had to be drilled out of his own cement sarcophagus. It was the rig's own hand tools that were used for the purpose.

It was the last drilling that the rig would ever do in Foxhole Down.

Jamie was briefly interviewed by the police, but the caved-in, severed head under the cricket pavilion was proof enough that he was innocent. It was all the cops could do to stop tittering at the thought that he would even take on the murderous Russian. Jamie felt humiliated. It wasn't the first time he had been laughed at by the police.

He was growing to hate authority.

In the village, things were moving from the surreal to the bizarre. Anouska's film crew were all over the place like a rash, filming everything that didn't move – and a few people that still could. Villagers, crew and whores, all the citizens of this small metropolis couldn't help themselves. They were all drawn to the green like a magnet. They were videoing it, taking selfies of it, and generally wandering around in front of it in a daze.

They were walking in a polluted wonderland.

Anouska's helpers were also going from door to door to make sure that no one tried to clean anything up, not that many were trying. Rumours spread about an enormous insurance payout.

It was important to maintain the integrity of the crime scene.

Then something really really strange happened. The toxicology reports on the toxic sludge came back negative.

The toxic sludge wasn't toxic at all.

It appeared that they had been fracking with a fluid that wasn't even a fracking fluid. It was beyond strange. It was the talk of the green, as everyone assisted the whores in retrieving their personal belongings from the whorehouse. At least they had no further need of hazmat suits.

The whores took their hazmat suits with them. They left Foxhole Down in a minibus with nary a backward glance. They weren't a sentimental bunch.

The revelation about the non-toxic toxic sludge sent the metropolis into a spin. It had been bad enough thinking that something sinister was going on. Everyone was used to people having evil schemes in the pursuit of money. They all had a lifetime's experience of it. This peculiar evil was in pursuit of something else. It made the villagers, especially the incomers, nervous. No one knew where they stood any more. Their sensibilities had been well and truly offended.

'I'm not standing for it,' said one fellow. He was wearing an Anarchy in the UK t-shirt. 'It's bad enough fighting against developers.'

He had moved in to the new development ten years ago.

'Who are we dealing with here? Undevelopers?' He threw his hands in the air. 'I want something done!' he yelled. 'I demand to know who's messing with me. I want compensation!'

The incomers were as one on this. They all demanded that something be done, especially the compensation bit.

Antonia could see that they were beginning to turn into a mob. She led Jamie back into the pub. If there was going to be a riot, she wanted a seated view of it. With a drink in her hand.

'Three bounces. And then under the whorehouse,' said Jamie.

'Darling, we're free,' said Antonia. She squeezed his hand.

That thought hadn't yet occurred to Jamie. They were no longer on the run. Finally, their life was their own. It was a momentous notion.

Rooster was drinking heavily and peering out of the front window to reassure himself that his final cement job was as catastrophic as he thought it was.

'If that's the best I can make of a standard cement job, then I'm finished in this business. The man in charge of that mess is useless. I'm firing myself.'

'Me too,' said Grassy Knoll. 'I'm leaving the village.'

'Not because of me I hope?' said Jenny.

'No,' said Grassy. 'This place has changed forever. And so have I. It's time for me to get out there and take the fight to the enemy.'

'Who's the enemy?' said Jenny.

'I've no idea,' said Grassy Knoll.

'Will you marry us?' said Hamish.

'I'd be delighted to,' said the Vicar.

Hamish and Jenny held hands and kissed.

The Vicar and Alan held hands and kissed.

'I'm also available for Christenings,' the Vicar beamed.

'Maybe soon,' Jenny said.

'Maybe really soon,' said Antonia.

Jamie felt his legs wobble. His mouth must have dropped open, because everyone was laughing.

'That's fabulous news,' Jamie croaked.

Amidst the cheering, Hamish delivered his own bombshell.

'Ladies and gentlemen. I first came here as a fixer. I think we can all agree that the village has been well and truly fixed – and not in a way that any of us could have foreseen. I am now about to fix my last thing. And I guarantee you that it won't disappoint.'

Hamish paused for effect - in his best actorly fashion.

'Tonight at eight pm, on this green, the owner of Land of Hope and Glory Drilling shall be revealed.'

Chapter 38 - Land of Hope and Glory

A stage was hastily erected in front of the derrick and facing the pub. Chairs were laid out, enough for the entire village. Anouska's camera crew got into position. A small proscenium arch was thrown up, with a curtain. Portacabins with dressing-rooms arrived. There were big spotlights, some for the stage, others threw light onto the clouds. A public address system got up and running and began playing awful music from the 1980s. The Major got his barbeque up and running in front of the pub and was soon doing a brisk trade. There was even free candyfloss. What few local children there were, darted in and out of the equipment, although their parents kept them clear of the non-toxic toxic sludge just to be on the safe side. Crowds began to gather as the bush telegraph got going. This was not an insignificant achievement, given that the incomers barely spoke to one another.

For the first time in many a year, there was a carnival atmosphere in Foxhole Down. The atmosphere was so heady that the Vicar took up a collection - and did rather well. Whilst the incomers took the folding seats, the village regulars sat on benches at the back provided for them by the Major.

The show did not disappoint.

At 7:30 pm precisely, the music stopped. There was a small bang as a firework was set off, and then an enormous bang as it exploded above them as a glorious, multi-coloured rose. There were oohs, ahhs and applause. There then followed a troupe of highly talented acrobats, tumblers, fire breathers and the like. There were more oohs and ahhs. This was top grade entertainment. It was timeless, harking back to medieval, even Roman times. Hamish took to the stage in tights and declaimed some Shakespeare to warm applause. His "hey nonny nonnies" sent the children into fits of giggles.

This was the cue for some no-holds-barred Morris dancing, followed up by a superb folk group. As they chanted, a light show illuminated the petrified village behind them. It was pagan. It was odd. It was magical. But all of this was a mere prelude to the pièce de résistance.

It was a Punch and Judy show.

Naturally, this was a thoroughly politically incorrect version of the puppet show. Mr Punch was very loving towards Judy, who left him to care for the baby. The baby took a severe pounding before being turned into sausages.

The regulars got the allegory straight away.

'Mr Punch is Land of Hope and Glory drilling,' said Antonia.

'The baby is Foxhole Down,' said Jamie.

The lovable Henry the Horse got short shrift. Beaten to death. Joey the Clown announced "dinner time" which was the cue for the Crocodile and Punch to fight over the sausages. The Doctor tended to Mr Punch's wounds before being dispatched himself. This brought in the Policeman and then the Hangman, who was forced into his own noose. Judy came back to be fed the sausages and then to be killed. Finally the Devil himself showed up. Punch, though, was triumphant over all.

The children loved it. The adults weren't so sure.

'Everyone apart from Punch is Foxhole Down,' said Grassy Knoll.

'That's the way to do it!' Punch trilled.

The stage fell into darkness. The ruined village was lit up.

Hamish's voice boomed over the public address. 'And now, ladies and gentlemen, boys and girls, please put your hands together for the CEO of Land of Hope and Glory Drilling and the person responsible for everything.'

'It's Benjamin Latham,' said Alan.

'It's Vladimir Rokossovsky,' said the Vicar.

'It's Donald Trump,' said Jamie.

'It's Anouska de Gaulle!' said Hamish.

The regulars looked around. Anouska had slipped away in the darkness. There she was, on stage in a flamboyant coat, multi-coloured like Mr Punch, the ultimate trickster.

The village gasped.

Anouska then began the speech which would be relayed across the globe on countless TV channels and would be replayed millions of times on social media. It would be intercut with shots of the destruction she had wreaked. She would look wonderful. Her digital technicians would make sure of that.

'I am Land of Hope and Glory Drilling,' she began. 'This is a result of my ego. I was the one who bribed the politicians, the civil servants, the villagers and the media. I made sure that no word of this leaked out into the wider world. Until now. I hired the rig and the rancid drillcrew. I ploughed the village green up and turned it into an industrial nightmare. I made sure they drilled into a fault line and caused an earthquake. I pumped gas into the water supply. I faked the red gas leak. I brought in the one-legged man to blow Alan's house up. I turned the cricket pavilion into a whorehouse. I hired the whores. I did even better than that. I turned you all into whores.'

The villagers weren't arguing. Most were sure that there was going to be another big firework display.

'There was no gas here. There was never anything to frack. It was never about money because it was always about money. It turned out better than I could ever have hoped. I didn't count on the sheer ineptitude of the crew that couldn't even perform simple sums. Look at the mess they made. Look at it.'

Everyone looked. It was just the most incredible cemented mess imaginable. Truth be told, it was the most incredible cemented mess unimaginable. It was strangely beautiful too, looking haunting under the green and red lights.

'Why did I do this?' Anouska continued. 'Why? I did it because I had money. And that's the only justification needed in this world. I have the money and I can do what I want. There is no God. There is no morality. There is no environment. There is money and there is nothing else.'

Anouska left a long silence. She wanted to make her point.

'Do you like what money can do?' she asked.

Silence. The villagers were still waiting on the fireworks.

'I thought I was clever when I made people confront disappointment in an empty room. Wait until they confront this. Yes, we're not going to clean it up. We're not going to change a thing. We're going to charge people a fortune to come and see this. And every whore in the town will get a cut.'

This got a cheer.

Ladies and gentlemen, I give you my latest and greatest work of art. I give you: What the Frack?'

There was an explosion and Anouska disappeared in a puff of smoke. A laser show illuminated the ruins of the church and the houses and the cricket pavilion. And yes, there was a stupendous firework display for the world's first oil well as a work of art.

*

They came to Foxhole Down in their droves. Special buses had to be laid on to prevent congestion. Anouska's rectory was used as the visitor centre, full of interactive displays. The entire débâcle was explained in multi-media format.

Anouska herself moved back to the city. She had achieved more in Foxhole Down than she dared imagine. Grassy Knoll also left, looking for a fight. He didn't have to look far. The Vicar and Alan got married, with the Vicar presiding. It was a confused service in a damaged church, but the bishop was happy. The money was rolling in. The village had nominated Fletcher as their negotiator.

Fletcher didn't move anywhere.

The Major moved to Marbella, where he found his wealthy widow. He didn't need to sell the pub after all. It was doing a roaring trade. He got a manager to keep an eye on things. And he got Fletcher to keep an eye on the manager.

The happier Jennifer got, the shorter her name seemed to get. So, after a bit of a squabble about Hamish's duplicity, or even triplicity, J married him. They weren't well suited; soul mates never are. They were, however, deeply and permanently in love. In a confused service in a damaged church, the Vicar wed them.

Church attendance soared. Amidst the confusion, many incomers discovered God. Others, bizarrely, came simply because they thought church attendance was a way to protest against Anouska's commercialisation of the village, although they had been happy to take her money.

Vladimir Rokossovsky returned to Russia and made a thrilling killing on the paintings. Antonia was right; selling forgeries was so much more fun. Inspector Witcher's investigations revealed Benjamin Latham MP to be so caught up in scandal with Vladimir and others that he was banished to the place reserved for all of the country's worst scumbags: the House of Lords.

Inspector Witcher got his promotion, but he got no thanks.

Rooster retired unhappily to his large slice of Louisiana. His loved ones learned never to mention the word "cement" in his presence. The scurvy crew were broken up and returned happily to their various nefarious second careers.

Jamie and Antonia fled to Catalonia. It took Jamie a little while to get out of the habit of fleeing. They settled down to prepare for the arrival of their baby. Having spent so much of his life with his head in the clouds, it came naturally to Jamie to become a programmer on the internet Cloud. It was the kind of job you could do anywhere. And that suited Jamie just fine. Antonia kept in touch with the dodgy art dealers and dealt in dodgy art. In Spain there were lots of dodgy people with dodgy motivations. They were all adults. Anouska preyed on Antonia's mind, although she never mentioned that to Jamie. They kept in touch.

There was no oil beneath Foxhole Down. But the well made more money for the village than oil ever could. They struck rich in a way that only Anouska could have imagined.

The sleepy little Hampshire village didn't produce any hydrocarbons. It didn't require to have toxic chemicals pumped into its fissures. What the Frack? won the Turner Prize for Art.

The End

By the Same Author - as B.D McKay:

DRILLING, KILLING, LOVE, DRUGS & MUD

JAMIE CHIVERS' life turns around when a man with prospects comes into his local pub by mistake. He ends up on an oil rig in the North Sea – and a desperate industry gets a desperate man. Unfortunately, on Jamie's first shift, someone bludgeons the Toolpusher to death and tosses him into a mud pit. All hell breaks loose. There's a big party. A seafood buffet. Pavlova. Dominoes. Jamie falls in love and has his heart broken by a roustabout. The cops arrive.

What happens to the body isn't fit to be read on a Kindle.

As others crack up, Jamie finds himself gaining in strength. Will he solve the murder? Will the rig strike oil? Will true love prevail?

Drilling, Killing, Love, Drugs & Mud – what it takes to extract the black gold that powers and may destroy the planet.